# *The* ANONYMOUS STRANGER

# The Anonymous Stranger

SUSAN PEARSON NORDBY

TATE PUBLISHING
AND ENTERPRISES, LLC

*The Anonymous Stranger*


This novel is a work of fiction. Names, descriptions, entities, and incidents included in the story are products of the author's imagination. Any resemblance to actual persons, events, and entities is entirely coincidental.

The opinions expressed by the author are not necessarily those of Tate Publishing, LLC.

Published by Tate Publishing & Enterprises, LLC
127 E. Trade Center Terrace | Mustang, Oklahoma 73064 USA
1.888.361.9473 | www.tatepublishing.com

Tate Publishing is committed to excellence in the publishing industry. The company reflects the philosophy established by the founders, based on Psalm 68:11,
*"The Lord gave the word and great was the company of those who published it."*


*Cover design by Samson Lim*
*Interior design by Jomar Ouano*

Published in the United States of America

ISBN: 978-1-68319-045-5
Fiction / Romance / Military
16.06.08

This book is dedicated to my very best friend of fifty-four years, Sue #2, for understanding where I have been and where I am going and loving me all the same. I love you, friend!

May the Lord bless you and keep you.
May the Lord make his face shine down upon you.

# PROLOGUE

Two men in a brown-colored Marine Corp automobile pulled up in front of her house. She answered the door, and although she knew why they were there, she let them in anyway. They were here to tell her that her husband, Cpl. Mark Williams, was killed in action. How did she know? She had had a dream.

They came in and sat down.

"Mrs. Williams, on behalf of the Secretary of War and the United States Marine Corp, we are here to inform you of the untimely death of your husband, Mark Williams."

"I already know," Sara said.

"I don't understand. How do you know?"

"I had a dream. I loved him so much, and I knew he was dead. About ten days ago, I was sleeping, and in my dream, God told me to prepare myself for an upcoming notification. I know that sounds awful, but in a way, I feel it was God preparing me." Then Sara broke down and started to cry. "But

I didn't know it was real, until now." She continued to cry. "Oh my God, what will I do without him? He was my whole world. I worked so hard and saved so when he came home he would be proud of me. Now he will never know. Ooohhh..."

"Ma'am, is there someone we can call to come and be with you?" asked the officer.

"Yes, you can call my mother. Here is her number." At that, the wailing started again.

The chaplain was trying to comfort her, but the wailing didn't stop. He was talking about the Bible, and she could see his lips move but didn't know what he was saying. She was so mixed up. She was so calm when they came in the door, but now she couldn't get herself under control.

The officers sat with her until her mom and dad came into the small house. After talking with the officers, her mom and dad said good-bye and thanked them for coming by to let Sara know in person.

It was 1968. Sara and Mark had been married for two years. They were high school sweethearts, and why did he have to leave her now? He had been in Vietnam ten months. It had been four months since she had seen him on R&R in Hawaii. She was carrying his baby. Her mom told Sara she had to take it easy; she could not lose this baby. She had already lost one, and this one was Mark's only chance to carry on his blood.

"Sara, sit down," her mom told her. Sara did sit down but couldn't help herself.

She cried and cried well into the next eight days while they were waiting for the body to come home.

The escort picked her up to take her down to the funeral home. She walked in and saw him under glass. Why was he under glass? The escort explained that it was because of the length of time since death. She stood and talked to him. She wanted to know what had happened. He had only two months and twenty days, and then he would have been home. She was going to miss him so much, and this baby would never personally know his daddy!

The funeral, for lack of another word, was beautiful. There were flags and flowers everywhere. They did a 21-gun salute and a flag folding ceremony at the cemetery. Sara cried some more and was so weak she had to have her mother and dad help her down the hill.

It was during the reception at her mother's house that Sara realized she had not eaten all day. That was not good for the baby. When she got home, she set the flag next to Mark's picture and wondered what she should do next.

# 1

She filed all the necessary papers for her widow's pension and her life insurance. There were bits and pieces also due, his last monthly check, combat pay, and hazardous duty pay. She would keep working for as long as she could, and then she would see if she could make it on her allotments. With the life insurance, she paid off the balance of the house, which was six thousand five hundred dollars. The total cost was eleven thousand dollars, and she had already paid four thousand five hundred dollars when she bought out her sister and brother-in-law. That would eliminate a house payment. Everything extra that she could over the next three months, she would put away. She would not buy one thing she did not need.

Her house was tiny, about a thousand square feet. It had three bedrooms, one bathroom, a living area, an eating area, and a tiny U-shaped kitchen. The walk-in pantry also housed the washer and dryer. But the yard was big, with lots of room for little Marcie or Mark Junior to play in. Her little house was cozy and comfortable, and she planned on living there as long as possible. She had started fixing up one of the bedrooms as the baby room and one room as her sewing room, which also had a desk in it for paying bills.

Sara was still devastated, and she found herself starting to cry. She would take big deep breathes of air, gulp it in even, just to breathe. She needed to get so she could go back to work and put in her day without crying all the time. They would be embarrassed for her if she cried all the time. So Sara started stuffing her feelings down deep inside each time she was with anyone else. But when she was alone, she got out her pictures and tried to imagine what her baby would look like.

The months passed, and the leaves were falling after having turned gold, red, and brown. Her due date was October 29. She worked just as long as they would let her. Then she stayed home and made baby clothes and diapers. Her sister, Sadie, gave her a baby shower, which was great. She got a stroller, which she really wanted, rubber pants, rattles, and receiving blankets, and her mom had knitted a full-crib-length blanket, and it was gorgeous. She was really excited about this little one.

She got busy and got all her thank-yous done right away. She washed all the clothes and hung them out in the September air on the clothesline located in her backyard. She was as ready as she could be. Sara got a couple of books at the library and would pass the time after her housekeeping was done by reading. She really enjoyed reading. Her water broke on the evening of October 28. She called her mom and dad, and they came right over and took her to the hospital. Little Mark Williams, Jr. was born at eleven thirty in the morning on October 29, 1968. She was so happy it was a boy to carry on his name. Sara had put their wedding picture on her built-in bookshelf beside one of her favorite pictures of Mark, sitting in front of a pup tent and eating out of a can of chili she had sent him. He may not know his daddy, but he would know what he looked like.

Sara's mom came and stayed a few nights with her, just until her stitches healed a little. It was hard to move around the first few days. Each day she got better and better. In the meantime, she learned she would not have to go back to work. She would have to be frugal, but that was okay. She had everything she needed for now, and the other stuff she would work on. Now that little Mark was born, she could file papers to increase the amount she would receive each month. They would be okay.

In the summer, Sara would take him out onto a blanket on the grass and let him crawl around. She would put some cars down for him, his rattle, and any other noisemaker she could find. Measuring spoons, that was always a good one.

When his first birthday came, she had a little party for him with family. They brought him presents and laughed and laughed when he got chocolate cake all over his face from his piece of cake. Oh, what a mess!

She would shop the thrift stores for little jeans and shorts for him, shirts, and jackets. She did not have the money to go buy brand-new. But he was a little guy and did not know the difference yet anyway.

Some of her friends wanted to set her up with one of their friends. She was even offered to double date, but the answer was always no. She just wasn't interested.

The Vietnam War was still going on, and the nightly news was full of those KIA (killed in action). She felt bad for all those mothers and widows who were going to be receiving the same sad news she herself had received. How long was this war going to go on anyway?

When Mark Junior turned two, Sara started to call him MJ. It was 1971, and the wound of losing his daddy was still prevalent to Sara. She just couldn't figure out how she could get beyond all of this grief. Would she ever or would she be sentenced to a life of constantly remembering. Maybe she should take her friends up on that dating offer.

Her days were filled with cleaning the house, laundry, cooking, baking, and taking care of MJ. He was so beautiful, and she was so happy to have him. Maybe that was part of the pain, the constant reminder since he looked so much like his daddy. They would take walks up to the park and play on the playground equipment.

Sara and little Mark Junior were at the park down the street from the house. He had turned three and loved to play on the playground. She had always heard that when you lost someone you loved very much, you would see someone who would look like them, or hear music that would remind you of them or smell something like a bakery that would remind you.

They were down at the park when Sara looked up and saw a guy standing behind a tree, looking at her. She saw a man who looked a lot like Mark Sr. He was about the same height and coloring. It made her shiver. She grabbed up little MJ and put him on her hip, and then she started to walk toward this man. Suddenly, he was nowhere to be seen. What had happened to him? She got chills. She knew Mark was dead; she had seen him in the coffin. She had been at his funeral and saw the coffin as it was being lowered into the ground. The man she saw was just her imagination, she was sure.

# 2

Sara and MJ would take walks over to her Mom and Dad's. They were wonderful grandparents and loved him dearly. Her dad always stepped up and tried to fill the shoes of the missing daddy. He wanted to protect little MJ so much from what had happened. It was not MJ's fault that his daddy had been killed in the war.

"Hey, buddy, how's Grandpa's little boy today?"

"I got a goldfish, Grandpa! I named him Buddy, after what you call me all the time."

"Oh my goodness, well, what do you plan to do with this little fish?" Grandpa asked.

"I am going to keep the bowl clean and feed him every day. I can talk to him and have him follow my finger on the glass," replied MJ.

"Well, I think that is pretty special. Grandma and I will have to come over to see the fish," said Grandpa, laughing and taking his hand and ruffling MJ's hair.

"Sara, what are you guy's planning this afternoon?" asked her dad.

"I thought we would make a trip to the library. As you know, he loves to be read to, and we are out of decent reading material at the moment. The ones we have, have been read and read," answered Sara.

"Well, that does sound fun. Hey, buddy, how do you feel about coming back here after the library and spending the night? Grandma and I miss you so much. You could bring some of your new books, and we will read them to you," asked Grandpa.

"Sure, Grandpa. That would be fun! Mommy, can I?"

"Okay, all right," Sara said.

"Let me slip by the house on the way back over here and get him some jammies and fresh clothes for tomorrow. "What about dinner? Do you want me to feed him before we come back?"

"No. In fact, why don't you both stay for dinner? I have a new recipe I have been dying to try out," said her mom.

"Well then, I guess we will see you after a while," said Sara.

It was fun adventure for her son, but not so fun for her. Sara was even sadder when she left. She felt that she was wrapping up too much of her life in her son. Doting a little too much and not taking care of what she wanted to take care. She would be truly lonesome without him tonight, and she wondered what she could do to keep herself busy.

Her dad handed her a twenty-dollar bill and told her to go by a few things for herself. She said thanks. Then he handed her a second twenty-dollar bill and told her to keep this one for groceries, which was where the first twenty-dollar bill would have gone if he didn't stop it from happening.

She laughed and told her dad that he knew her too well.

She and MJ went to the library and then to the house to pick up the necessary items, and then she dropped back at her mom and dad's. Afterward, she left to go to the house but decided at the last minute that she would use some of the money if she could find a couple of things she needed at the thrift store.

She perused the aisles of clothing and came up with a pair of jeans, two blouses, and a new cardigan for a total of ten dollars. She tried everything on and was very happy with the way they fit. *Thank you, Dad*, she thought.

She went on home and opened a can of soup, made a grilled cheese sandwich, and ate. She hated being by herself. It was like she had no value as a human being. She decided to work on her scrapbook of MJ. She got out the books onto the table and started to look through them. She thanked God every day for him, even when he was a stinker going through the terrible twos and the awful threes. She was ever so happy she had him, was able to go full term in her pregnancy and not miscarry like the first baby.

She was looking at the first book, the one where she was pregnant at her baby shower. She had put the letter she had received back from Mark where he had found out she was pregnant and how happy he was. He loved the idea of starting a family and was looking forward to coming home and seeing her big round belly. She chuckled a little at the thought.

The last page she turned to was when MJ was three and a half years old. She hadn't seen that man that looked like Mark in over six months. It must have been her imagination. She began to work on the time from where she left off and now. She hummed and pasted. She cut and matched her sayings with the picture. Soon she was all caught up, putting her things away because her favorite TV program would soon be on. It felt funny to go to bed without MJ in the house. She knew it was no protection, but he was company. She made sure the doors and windows were all locked before crawling into her comfy comforter and pillows. She would go pick up MJ first thing in the morning.

The wind had come up sometime during the night. She awoke with a start as the wind blew a branch, scraping back and forth across the window. Sara looked out the window, determined the noise to be the branches and cuddled back up under her covers. Suddenly, she sat straight up. She had seen a man looking through her window. She was sure of it. She got out of bed and went to the phone. She dialed 911 and told them that she had a Peeping Tom looking through her windows. They sent a car out immediately. They knew who was calling and tried to take care of the single women in each neighborhood. One went to the door, while the other one walked around the house.

"Hello, Mrs. Williams. Sorry you have had a disturbance tonight."

"Officer, it was so spooky. I looked out my window and saw the silhouette, and it scared me. I am actually glad you didn't find anything," said Sara.

"Can you describe what you saw, Mrs. Williams?"

"Yes, a man, I am sure of it because of the outline of the haircut. Today with all the guys having longish hair, I would say it would be closer to a military cut. Other than that, it would be a side view, a silhouette. I am not sure I am much help. What woke me up was the wind blowing the branches against my window. I turned over to go back to sleep, and that is when I saw him."

"Let's go in the bedroom." They walked down the hall and were standing in her room. "Can you show me where on the window he came up to? That would give us a clue of the height."

Sara pointed to where on the window she thought the man came to. The other officer was on the outside, measuring the spot from the ground up. The officer talked to the inside officer through their walkie-talkies. "About six foot one inch, Joe," he said. *Mark was six foot one* inch, thought Sara. *Coincidence again, I am sure*. They took any additional information she had and then left. Sara made sure while the officers where still there that every window was locked and the back door double-locked. She double-locked the front door when they left.

A cup of chamomile tea, a good book, and her fuzzy blanket in her favorite chair and she was again set. If she fell asleep, this was where it would happen tonight.

# 3

Sara went on about her business and soon found herself going out once in a while. She felt like she was cheating. She felt like, for some reason, her husband wouldn't think she loved him anymore and that he would be angry with her. But she went anyway.

The first date she went on was a total disaster. He was a divorced man with five children. He had ten dollars to spend for the whole evening if he was lucky. He talked about his ex-wife the entire time. He complained about her. She spent all his money every time he got paid, within two days they were broke until his next payday. He didn't know what she did all day long because he would come home, do the dishes for the day, finish the laundry that she, at least, started, fold it, and put it away. He would write out checks for the next payroll before she could get her grubby hands on it. Then he complained, now that he was divorced, about how much child support and spousal support he had to pay. He was living in a room in a boarding house situation, and she had the big house. Something was not right here.

"Jerry, if things are worse without her, why don't you work to get back together?" asked Sara.

"I don't know, I just feel helpless. I feel like I am damned if I do and damned if I don't. Some of the grumbles come from the lack of lovemaking. She was too tired, she had a headache. Then, well, I found out that the 'too tired' was named Gregory, and the 'headache' was called Richard."

"So in other words, she was already cheating on you when you filed for divorce?"

"It looks that way. So what would you like to do tonight?"

"I would really like you to take me back home. I don't think I am ready to date yet," said Sara.

Jerry took her back home. When he walked her to the door, he tried to kiss her. Sara gently pushed him away, saying, "Jerry, it was really nice to meet you, and I wish you all the luck in the world, but I am really not ready for romance yet. Good night."

Sara went into the house, sat down on her chair, and started to laugh. She laughed and laughed—it was almost a hysterical laugh. If that was what dating was about, she definitely was not ready yet.

Another year went by, and MJ was now four. They went to visit his father's grave on Memorial Day and took flowers and a small flag. When they went home, MJ laid down for his nap, and Sara found herself digging out all the old photo albums and getting sentimental. She had a good walk down memory lane. She remembered their years in high school together and the first time she realized she had fallen in love with him. They had gone to both their junior and senior proms together. They had danced the night away, she in her long dress and Mark in his tux. She would never forget how romantic it was. They walked along the waterfront afterward and vowed their love for each other.

Two years later, they got married. She was still just nineteen, but Mark had turned twenty already. He had joined the Marines as a way of paying for college. Sara had taken business classes in high school and had every intention of working full time while Mark was put through college. That was another thing that didn't work out.

Sometimes she was very lonesome. Her friends had their husband and their families. While she had MJ, she didn't have a husband. She decided she would start to date again. It was time, she guessed.

Her second date since Mark was buried turned out to be actually fun. She went on a picnic with a friend of a friend. He had asked MJ to go to. They played catch, three-way catch, and it was fun. They hiked to a wooded area and then had lunch while leaning up next to some big logs lining a creek area. It was too cold to go wading, but in another month, it would be good. This man's name was Doug. She dated him several more times, and then he started pushing the sex thing. She wasn't ready yet. She still struggled with feeling guilty just being on a date and being intimate. Even though he was really nice, she broke it off just before MJ turned five.

Once MJ was in kindergarten, she was even lonelier. She could not make her child give her all the love she desired. So her friends introduced her to Joseph Christopher. He was a widower with a little girl, Lacey. She was a cutie! They would go out, the four of them, or they would go out as a couple. She enjoyed being around him and his little girl. He enjoyed her and little Mark. He would throw him up in the air and catch him, and MJ would laugh and laugh.

Joseph was a kind man. He had lost his wife to breast cancer. It was something she discovered when she had tried to nurse Lacey—it was already at stage three—and she died when Lacey was one year old. A couple of years later, Joseph started to date but never found anyone he wanted to make it permanent with. Until Sara.

Sara, on the other hand, started dating beyond Doug, two or three guys, but no one ever measured up, until Joseph.

They went to a steak house on their first date. The food was delicious, but the restaurant was also the kind that can take you hours to eat. They sat and visited about all sorts of things—their kids, how they lost their previous spouses, what kind of things they liked to do for fun, sports, their values as far as money, homes, and taking good care of what they owned. They found they had a lot in common.

They got the kids together the next time, and they were great friends from the beginning. This was the first time Sara had dated anyone with children, and it was rather scary. Not only was she risking everything falling in love with this girl's daddy, but she was also taking on the responsibility of two individuals for the rest of her life if they ended up marrying.

They would go on picnics and long drives with the kids. Sometime they would go camping on the beach, and even in state and federal campgrounds. They would take vacations and go to the Grand Canyon and Yellowstone National Park. They went out on dates to the movies and to dinner, and they never were at a loss for words. They were always talking with each other about all sorts of things.

That was the one thing that made Sara think seriously about Joseph. What a really good friend he had become and how they just had so much fun together, even when they were sitting watching TV or working in the yard together.

They dated for three years and decided to get married—something she thought she would never do. But it had been eight years by this time. She saw the anonymous stranger every once in a while, but when she went to talk to him, he always disappeared. Was it just a coincidence, or was he a stalker?

One time when she saw him, she sat and stole looks as sneakily as possible. She was sitting at a playground with Lacey and MJ, wearing dark glasses. She would point her head one way and her eyes another. After a while, she started getting a headache. She just couldn't stop staring. He looked so much like Mark, but that was impossible. She never did tell Joseph. She was finally happy after eight years, and nothing was going to take that away.

They kept Sara's house and used it as a rental. They sold Joseph's house and purchased one that would be their own. It was the beginning of a new history. It was about double the size of her house. She knew she would be spending hours every day cleaning and doing laundry, but that was okay; she was happy to do it. She did love Joseph, not the same kind of love she had with Mark, more a secure love. They had a great time together and had become great friends. She didn't want any other children, but he did, so she convinced him to wait awhile.

The house they decided on was actually more than two thousand square feet on two floors. It had a daylight basement. The main floor had three bedrooms, two bathrooms, a kitchen, a dining room, and a living room. Downstairs were laundry, family room, another bathroom, and a small bedroom that Sara would use as her sewing room. They lived three blocks from the grade school and middle school and a half mile from the high school. It would make a nice home for both of their children to grow up in.

Both children were in the wedding. Lacey was her maid of honor, and Mark was Joseph's best man. They were too young to sign the wedding certificate, so Joseph lined up a couple of other witnesses to sign the marriage certificate. She suddenly got very nervous and would miss having her own money and the independence that she had claimed. Was she doing the right thing by saying yes to marrying him?

Her dress was a short white dress and lacey like a semiformal you would wear in high school. As a matter of fact, she found it at Value Village and assumed it was either a prom dress or a winter formal dress. Lacey was dressed in a lavender dress, which was very pretty. The wedding was beautiful, and then everyone came back to their house for a potluck reception. It worked out well. Sara's mom and dad really liked Joseph and felt he would do a good job in taking care of her. As they walked out of the church, she saw that man standing by his car, looking at her. Man, he sure did look like Mark Sr. She shook her head. *Impossible, but, man…*

She and Joseph were going to her house to party and then on a quick four-day honeymoon to Reno, Nevada. They got up the next morning and cleaned the house after the party, got their suitcases, and drove nine hours to Reno. They had two days left before they were going to have to drive nine hours back. First thing Sara did when she saw a slot machine was put a quarter in it. It clanged, and bells rang as she had won twenty-five dollars. Well, good start. Or beginner's luck.

Joseph went up to the room to take a nap. All that driving just about did him in. Sara saw that man. What the heck was he doing here in Reno? She could have sworn it was him. He had on a dark leather jacket, and his hair was darker, like it had been oiled down. But she was sure it was him. What would he be doing here anyway? Why was he following her? She started to walk toward him, and he walked away very fast. Okay, this was starting to irritate her. She followed in the direction he had left, but she couldn't see anyone. Was it her imagination again?

They had a fun time in Reno. They played a few slots, took in a show, and drove up to Virginia City and had their picture taken in old time Western gear. She was a saloon lady, and Joseph was a sheriff. It would definitely be something to always remember.

They got home, Joseph went to work on Monday, and she set up the house for real. She opened boxes of wedding presents and wrote each note before putting away the gift. That way she always knew where she was with her thank-yous. She loved her kitchen. It was a modernized U shape, similar to the one she had at the small house, but this one was larger and had much more cupboard space. They had purchased from the people who had lived there before them a china hutch and a beautiful table. Sara got very busy and had the hutch all cleaned up inside and out. The table was waxed, and about 65 percent of the gifts were put away with the thank-yous written.

"Hey, Mom, how was your day?" asked MJ.

"Very good. I am trying to organize this kitchen and the buffet here in the dining room. I want to ask you something. Do you remember ever seeing the same man more than once standing behind a tree or a car?"

"No, why, Mommy?" asked MJ.

"Oh, I just wondered is all. Do you want a snack before Lacey comes home?"

"No thanks, I will wait for Lacey. We can eat together." Then he bounced off toward his bedroom.

It was no more than a half hour later when Lacey arrived.

"Whatcha doin'?" asked Lacey.

"Trying to get organized is all," replied Sara.

"Oh, I thought you were making a mess," said Lacey.

"Nope, that's when I cook," Sara said as a little chuckle came up from deep inside of her.

"Well, I think you are a good cooker. Really sometimes my daddy would make awful stuff, and I would hurt his feelings by telling him, 'No, how about a pizza?'"

"Thank you, Lacey, that means a lot to me!" said Sara with a huge smile on her face. Progress!

"Would you and MJ like a snack?"

"Yes, please. I am starving."

"Well, okay then. Here you go." She passed two plates to her, one for her and one for MJ. "You both have applesauce muffins, and I will follow you and bring the milk."

"Thanks, Mo—I mean Sara," said Lacey.

Sara ran the milk downstairs and came back up to work on her project. Her skills clicked in, and she had the kitchen done in no time, along with the fire extinguisher hung up on the wall. There was even some more room for wedding presents. She still had lots and lots to do to get them moved in and settled, but for now it was time to get her dinner cooking.

She stood by her front window and stretched. It had been a very busy day. And tomorrow she would go to the post office to take her thank-yous so far and get some extra stamps so she could mail the rest when they were written. She glanced down the street and saw a suspicious car. Inside was a man. This time she walked out her front door and down the street. She got closer this time, but just as she was getting there so she could get a good look, he pulled his visor down and revved up the engine. Next time she would call the police. But what would she tell them? This guy that looked like her first husband had been sitting in a car? Oh, brother, best to forget it.

# 4

Lacey and MJ really liked each other and played well together—Mark was in third grade, and Lacey was in fifth—maybe because of the fact that they weren't really related, no blood involved to get in the way with sibling competitions. One was younger, one older, one boy, one girl; that was why she didn't want more children. Lacey and MJ were great friends. Lacey got MJ to sometimes play dolls, and MJ got Lacey to sometimes play cars. So far so good.

Joseph came home from a long day at work. As he walked in, he smelled dinner and got a big smile on his face.

"Yum, it smells so good. What are we having?" he asked.

"Well, it is a creamy chicken casserole I saw in my magazine not too long ago. We had all the ingredients left over from a previous meal, so I thought, hmm, time to try a new recipe," answered Sara.

"I appreciate all you do for this family, Sara."

"I appreciate you going to work so I don't have to. I can stay home, keep the house clean, do laundry, take care of the kids, and the many more things I can't think of right at this moment."

"Sara, you make me laugh, but it is so nice to come home to a clean house, with dishes done, dinner cooked, and clean clothes in the closet, ironed even," said Joseph.

"I love doing it for you, Joseph. Really it is an honor!"

They spent the rest of the evening, after dinner, working in the yard for a few hours. Joseph mowed the lawn, and Sara got down on her hands and knees and went through the flowerbeds and pulled weeds and fluffed the dirt, readying it for bark dust. It was a good feeling to work together. It was fun, and by the time the lawn was cut and edged, it was time to go in, as it was starting to get dark. She got MJ in the bathtub, while Lacey took a shower in their bathroom. She turned down their beds and gave them each a kiss good night. The rule was they could read for fifteen minutes, and then it was lights out.

There was a time she never thought she would be content again, but she would have to say she felt contentment now. They led a quiet life, but it was also nice.

Tomorrow after she finished the wedding thank-yous, she would put the family room together, so she and Joseph went to bed a little earlier than usual. They got a good night's sleep.

The next morning, Sara got up and got breakfast on the table for everyone. They had French toast and bacon, orange juice, and coffee. Lacey gave her a hug and thanked her for the breakfast. She said when it was just her and her dad, most mornings was boxed cereal.

"Thanks, Mo—Sara," said Lacey.

"You know, Lacey, anytime you feel comfortable calling me Mom, I would be honored. I realize I could never replace your mother, but we could call it a nickname if you wish."

"Oh, thanks, Mom. I love you," said Lacey as she raced to give Sara another big hug.

"You are welcome, daughter!" said Sara as Lacey was beaming from ear to ear.

So it was settled—they were mother and daughter. MJ was already calling Joseph Dad, so now they were truly a family.

School continued the rest of the spring, and then school was out for the summer. She wasn't sure what she was going to do with the kids at home each day all day long, but she would put on her imagination cap and think of some things.

One thing they decided to do was find out how much it would cost to get a swimming pass for the summer for each of them. On Wednesdays, she sat down with the newspaper advertisements and had the kids cut out all the coupons, whether she ended up using them or not. They went for bike rides outside of the neighborhood for a couple of miles each way. It was good for them to get some exercise. Otherwise, if they stayed pretty much in front of the house, they could ride their bikes without her. The kids would play ball, kickball, and softball. There were also trips to the library each week.

When the kids were outside, Sara used that time to do laundry, hang it out, iron, and cook meals. Sometimes it would be barbecued hot dogs, cantaloupe and grapes, and ice cream cones for dessert. She loved summertime. Watermelon, cupcakes, barbecued hamburgers—easy. MJ came in and told her there was a man looking at them from down the street. Sara ran out the door toward the car. She got close enough this time that she yelled at the man.

"What do you want? What do you want with my family? Should we be afraid of you? Who are you? You look like my first husband, yet I know that can't be because I saw him in the coffin and saw the coffin go in the ground! Answer me, what do you want?" Sara yelled all these rapidly as she was walking toward the car.

"Sorry, ma'am, my mistake. I won't bother you again," said the man.

"Then get out of here and don't come back!" yelled Sara.

"Yes, ma'am. I am gone."

Sara started crying; she was so frustrated. Who was he anyway, and why did he look like Mark Sr.? If he was a brother or a twin, you would have thought he would have come forward long ago. So that wasn't it. She would watch out for him again.

# 5

Several months passed, and she never saw him again. She and Joseph worked in the yard each night, planting flowers and then bark dust. It looked so pretty when they got done. What a great accomplishment. She asked Joseph if she could have a vegetable garden. They had a cherry tree, an apple tree, and a pear tree in their yard already, and she thought a vegetable garden would be wonderful. Joseph rented a rototiller to dig up the area. MJ and Lacey raked all the clots out and helped plant the seeds. There was corn, green beans, tomatoes, lettuce, cucumbers, zucchini, and carrots. This would be a fun adventure for the kids too.

Throughout the summer, Sara kept looking up and down the street and over her shoulder but did not see the man anywhere. Good, maybe he was out of her life now.

August and September—the two best canning months—came. They had already made strawberry, raspberry, marionberry, and blackberry freezer jams. So now they were going to can corn, green beans, dill pickles, tomatoes, zucchini relish, and carrots. They also canned cherries, chunky applesauce, and pears. It was a fun summer after all, and though they would can in the morning before it got too hot and go swim in the afternoon, it was great to have the kids help her.

School started, and MJ was in the fourth grade, while Lacey was in sixth grade. Next year she would go to middle school. *Oh my goodness, they are growing up way too fast*, she thought.

"How was school today?" asked Sara.

"There's going to be a fall dance by the name of Sadie Hawkins. It is where the girl can ask the boy to dance but is only for six graders," said Lacey between bites of toast. "Yum. I am so glad you married my dad. I have tasted such delicious food."

"Thank you, Lace. You just mix cinnamon and sugar and put it into this container with holes on the top and then sprinkle over buttered toast. So tell me more about this dance."

"Well, the thing is a guy I like is named Mike. But we can't ask them to be our date, only to dance when it is time."

"Is the dance at night?" asked Sara.

"No, it is after lunch for the rest of that day in the gym. There will be bales of hay and scarecrows for decorations."

"Should I volunteer to be a chaperone?"

"No, that's okay. You could volunteer for cookies or punch if you wanted."

"Okay, I can do that. Who do I call?"

She made six dozen cookies for the dance. Sara went to a craft store and got cookie cutters for pumpkins, scarecrows, and black birds. She made sugar cookies one day and then spent the next two decorating them. They looked really cute, if she did say so herself. Well, only until Lacey walked in and saw the finished product.

"Mom, these are the most beautiful cookies I have ever seen," said Lacey with big eyes.

"Lacey, you are so worth it, honey. I was happy to do it for you."

"Mom, I am going to do the dinner dishes tonight so you can sit with your feet up. You deserve it!"

"Why, Lacey, that is really sweet of you. I'll take you up on it, and then I will tell you how much fun I had doing it."

"It's okay, Mom. You still deserve it."

She packed the cookies for delivery in the morning for the dance. Sara thought she just might be as excited as Lacey. The kids got to wear cutoff jeans, and Lacey would look really cute. She was cute anyway with her long blond hair, hazel eyes, and huge smile. Sara felt really lucky to have such a good kid for a stepdaughter. She had heard horror stories, but so far none had come true for her.

She got the kids in the car as well as the cookies and then was set to go. The kids ran in through the front doors, and Sara followed behind, laughing. She glanced into the principal's office to see who Mrs. Calley was talking to. She stopped dead in her tracks—from behind, he looked like Mark. The cookies were getting heavy, so she decided to take them on to room 205 and deliver them. Then she would return to see what she could find out about the guy in the principal's office.

"Hello," said Miss French.

"Hello," said Sara. "How is everything going? Are you as ready for the dance as the kids are?" asked Sara.

"One thing you have to remember, Mrs. Christopher, is that the kids at this age are all excited until the actual dance. Then they suddenly all get shy. It's hard to get them out on the dance floor to mingle, chat with one another, even eat. The boys have no problem eating, but the girls don't want to be seen as fat, so they don't eat."

It was a good thing that Sara had decorated a dozen more cookies just for the kids and for her husband. When she got back to the principal's office, she found the perspective Mark gone…and Mrs. Calley too. Well, she would catch her next time.

The cookies had been a big hit at the dance that day, and pretty Lacey didn't sit down once but was always out on the dance floor. She came home all excited and told Sara all about it. Mike was the one who asked her to dance most, and she was so animated in telling her about it. Sara was so happy their relationship was good.

It was close to Christmas, and Sara was busy making cookies. She was looking at magazines in the store, trying to decide which one she would like to try for new recipes. She saw a picture of a man with a beard. Chills went down her spine again. The man looked like the man who had been spying on her. She read that this person was in a band. Mark had played guitar. His hair was also longer than normal. It was kind of hard to recognize him, but she knew it was him. She bought that magazine not because of the recipes but because of that man's picture. The whole thing was a mystery to her.

She got home and hid the picture in her underwear drawer, one place that Joseph never went to. She got busy with loading the washer and dryer and getting out the ingredients for the cookies she wanted to start with. They were going to have a Christmas open house with their neighbors so they could meet more of them. She had met a few while out working in the yard but not near enough. She saw people crossing to one another's houses all the time, and she wanted to be one of them.

She folded clothes and put them away and then did clothes from washer into the dryer next. She finished her one batch of cookies and let them cool thoroughly. She then put them in baggies and took them out to the garage to the freezer. It was a coffee-cookies-desserts-punch kind of open house.

Sara made two more batches that day, always thinking of Mark. How she missed him, how she had loved him. Would she never be able to get away from thinking about him all the time? She started dinner just as everyone started to roll in. MJ and Lacey were both on the same start and release times now that they were a little older. They came on in, and Sara let them have their choice of two cookies and a glass of milk for an after-school snack. She told them to go change their clothes and start their homework while she was starting dinner.

She had made a pork roast, mashed potatoes, gravy, green beans from their garden, applesauce from their apple tree, and green salad. For dessert, they each had a couple more cookies. Out of the three recipes, they voted which one they liked first, second, and third. It was really good information, and Sara decided she needed to search for other recipes.

Their home was quite cozy during the holidays. The Christmas tree was up and in the front window. There were arrangements on each end table (smaller ones) and a larger one with several candles for the coffee table. There was also fire in the fireplace, making it warm and cozy. Sara had a knack for decorating, so everything always looked nice. They were on a pretty tight budget if Sara was to stay at home, so she would pick up some pretties at garage sales and thrift stores. Downstairs was another fireplace, couch set, and the TV. There was also Sara's old furniture, but again it was decorated so it looked very festive and definitely cozy.

The day of the open house came, and the kids were all dressed nice—Lacey in a dress and warm stockings and MJ in a button-down long-sleeved shirt and nice slacks. MJ opened the door when the guests arrived, and Lacey took their coats to their bedroom to lay on the bed. The eggnog was made (no alcohol), the cranberry and seven-up were prepared (with some rum), and a coffeepot with decaf coffee was on the kitchen counter. Sara had made one dessert where she used prepackaged sugar cookies and cherry pie filling, which were delish and also very Christmassy with the red and white. She had different candies on her table, intermingled with the platters of cookies. There were signs in front of the punch bowls so that someone wouldn't get the wrong stuff by mistake.

It was really a fun evening. They met almost everyone in the neighborhood. Sara knew exactly which one she would make friends with next. She was a lady who had a happy smile on her face the whole party, and she made Sara feel so welcomed into the neighborhood. Her name was Lucy Hamilton, and she was a kick in the pants, always positive. Sometime during the evening, Lucy brought up her shopping at Meier and Franks. She said she shopped only their red tag sale, but then with one coupon, she could get an additional 20 percent off. Then she said she waited until the day when they would have an additional 15 percent off on top of other coupons. She said she walked out of the store with a huge shopping bag full of clothes for thirty-seven dollars. Sara couldn't believe it. She said she would take her next time and show her how it was done. Sara said that would be great. She also taught Sara about double couponing and how to make something out of hardly anything at all. It was the beginning of a great friendship.

Sara kept very busy every day—cleaning, laundry, cooking—and she enjoyed every moment of it. It had always been her dream to be a stay-at-home mom. When Mark was killed, she had worked out a budget so that she could stay home with her little guy. She received a widow's pension that was discontinued when she got married to Joseph. She also received a social security payment for MJ, and that would continue until he was eighteen. The same was received for Lacey by Joseph. She worked very hard to make her dollar stretch back then, but what she was learning from Lucy was pretty good stuff. She would slip down every few days and have a quick cup of coffee with Lucy. Or Lucy would come up to her house.

Lucy took a yard of fabric and a drinking glass and traced as many circles as she could make on this fabric. Then she took her scissors and cut out each circle. From the backside, she took her iron and turned down one eighth of an inch and pressed it all around. Then she took cotton lace and put around the edge. These made darling coasters—for cheap. She gave each household six or eight, depending on how many lived in the household. She made a fudge that Sara loved, which was so creamy, and made tons and tons. She was a good friend to have, and she definitely had many talents besides being a very nice lady.

One day, she told Lucy about seeing this guy that looked a lot like her first husband who was killed in Vietnam. Lucy told her that was pretty normal. She took a grief recovery class when she lost her dad, and they said that other people start looking like, or reminding you of, the person you lost. Smells and sounds such as music could also remind you of the person.

Sara said to Lucy, "So do you think it is part of my imagination? In other words, you think I am just imagining him?"

"No, Sara, now settle down. I was not saying anything of the kind. I was just passing on what I learned. If you want to believe that this guy is Mark. Then believe it."

"Lucy, I don't know what to believe. I saw him in the casket. I saw him under this stupid glass that they put over the guys to encase them because they had been dead for seven to fourteen days before they could get shipped home. His face was puffy, and he didn't look like himself then, but he does now. Tell you what, next time I come down to see you, I want you to take a look at a couple of pictures. Will you do that for me?"

"Sure. Hey, I don't want you going and getting all upset about this. I just feel that if he is dead, he is dead."

"Okay, well, I had better go anyway because I need to get dinner going for the family. Thanks, Lucy, for the coffee. Next time I will bring us some cookies to munch on while we take a look at a couple of pictures," said Sara, a small amount of sarcasm still evident in her voice. It was like she was hurt for some reason. She couldn't put her finger on it. She was going out on a limb telling Lucy about the anonymous stranger, and then to have Lucy preach to her kind of hurt her.

She went to her bedroom and got the picture with the long hair and beard. Then she pulled a couple of pictures when they were first married, the wedding. She felt she should be able to tell the difference.

Sara got busy and fixed a snack for the kids when they walked in the door. Then she started dinner on the stove—a pot roast with potatoes, carrots, onion, celery and the magic touch, onion soup mix. That was what gave it a great flavor. She got out the ironing board and ironed a couple of Joseph's work shirts, three to be exact. She then took them to the bedroom to put into his side of the closet and then ironed two work slacks. She used a spray starch so they would look and stay crisp. She wanted him to look very nice every day. She was anxious to start a knitting class. She wanted to do cardigans for herself and Lacey and learn how to do men's sweaters. She was going to try making some of those coasters that Lucy had made to give to her family and Joseph's, just a little something.

She took the slacks to put them away and was looking out the window when she noticed his car. She wanted to get a picture of him. She took her camera, but then it wouldn't enlarge enough, so she ran down the hall to the hall closet to retrieve Joseph's camera. It had a long-range lens. She took it back to the bedroom and zoomed in on him. She snapped about five pictures as close up as she could get them. By looking through the lens, it seemed as though you could see who was sitting there. She just stood and watched him, and here came Lacey and MJ walking down the street. He didn't do anything to harm them; he just watched. That was it. he just watched the boy.

# 6

The next day, when Sara was out getting some groceries, she dropped the film off. It would be ready in three days. She bought a couple of new rolls of film for the camera. She did not tell Joseph that she had used it and wanted to get the camera reloaded as soon as possible. She hoped she could do it okay. It was a pretty fancy camera. When she got home, she got the camera and discovered all you had to do was set the film inside the camera, push a button, and then it would auto-reload. She called Lucy and told her she was going to wait a couple of days until she came down with pictures. Everything was all right; she just needed to be at home the next few days.

Three days passed, and she went to pick up the film. They were a little blurry, but you could see the long hair and the long beard. It spooked her out even more. She took everything down to Lucy and presented her case. She showed Lucy the first pictures, their marriage, etc. Then she showed her the picture in the magazine and the five pictures that she took.

"Wow, I can see why you think this guy might be Mark. He does resemble him quite a bit," said Lucy.

"Well, one thing to remember is that there is almost ten years between those pictures of us getting married and the one where he has longer hair and beard. Of course, he is going to look a little older, change a little," said Sara.

"Sara, I really want what you want. If you say this guy is Mark, then let's figure this out. How could it be? If you saw him in the coffin, then you know it was Mark and that they didn't bury someone else. I don't get it either. This is truly a mystery!"

Sara was pacing up and down the kitchen at this point. "Would the military pretend he was dead for some reason when he really wasn't?"

"Stop and think about that for a second, Sara. Why would Mark go along with the military on that scheme when he knew you were pregnant? He would want to be home with the baby, wouldn't he?"

"Well, I would think so. I just can't imagine what would make Mark do something like that. I just don't understand either. For now, I just want to let it go. This whole thing is not fair to Joseph. He is the one I am married to at the present."

"I think that is a really good idea," said Lucy, getting up to let her friend out the door and giving her a hug when they reached the door.

The next day was the last day of school before Christmas vacation. Hopefully the snow would hang around so they would have a white Christmas. Sara loved white Christmas.

It was so clean and beautiful with the lights dancing on the snow, catching the light like the snowflakes as if they were diamonds. It truly was beautiful.

She started dinner when she got back; a roasted chicken, cheesy potatoes, green salad, and a vegetable—she hadn't decided which one yet. She would take the rest of the chicken leftover, take it off the bone, and use it for tomorrow night's dinner, Chicken Rice-a-roni Soup. She would make biscuits to serve with the soup, and she would let the children decide if they wanted strawberry, raspberry, or marionberry jam. *Yum*, she thought. She was hungry for the soup, but it was still a day away.

# 7

The man unlocked his room and turned around as he took off his coat. It was a small room, barely big enough for a queen-size bed, a small dresser, a chair with an ottoman and a lamp. On top of the dresser was a one-burner stove element. Alongside the dresser was a very small refrigerator. One of the dresser drawers held a pan for soup, a fry pan for eggs, a plate, a bowl, and a cup. On top of the dresser was a box of cereal and instant coffee, and inside the refrigerator were some milk, eggs, and butter. There was a small closet, but then he didn't need much. He only had a few shirts, pants, and one other coat. There were a few other things he decided to hang on to in case he needed them.

On the nightstand was a picture of the beautiful lady. He had searched for her a long time, and now that he had found her, she was married and had a son—but wait, she had a son way back when he first found her. The boy looked like he was three or four years old back then. He looked very happy with his mommy.

She was the most beautiful woman he had ever seen. She was tall with reddish brown hair and blue gray eyes that twinkled when she smiled. Then there was that dimple in her left cheek. The glimpses he had taken soon would not be enough. He would have to go further but not without a plan.

He sat down at his one-person table, writing paper, and pen in front of him. He picked up the pen and started writing. He knew where she lived—check. He knew where her husband worked and his usual hours—check. He knew where her son and stepdaughter went to school, when they left and when they got home—check. He knew when she went to the grocery store, library, swimming in the summer, and not much else.

He had bought a pair of binoculars so he wouldn't have to park so close to the house. He just had to watch from varying parking spots. He sat and thought a long time about his next move, and finally it came to him.

# 8

Sara had never told Joseph about the man. It started at the playground when MJ was three, but then he seemed to disappear for a year or two and then came back. She kept the magazine picture and the five pictures she had taken with Joseph's camera hidden away in her underwear drawers. She just pretended it had never happened. He seemed to come up missing after she ran down the street like a banshee screaming at him. She had to laugh about it now. Whoever was inside that car must have thought, *Here she comes, that crazy lunatic again*.

"I had better get out of here before she hits me with a baseball bat or that dish towel she has in her hands." Sara laughed and laughed until tears flowed down her face.

And then she sobered. But why did he look so much like her first husband? Although thicker in stature, there was still a strong resemblance. She went to her bedroom and dug out the magazine picture. The name of the band was Happy

Tears, and they played every night except on Sundays and Mondays. She took the information into the other room and called information for the club's phone number. She called the number and asked what time the band started playing. They told her it was nine o'clock and that tonight was ladies' night.

"What does that mean?" Sara asked.

"It means ladies drink free."

"Really, no cost?"

"There is a cover charge though."

"How much is that, please?" asked Sara.

"It is five dollars for the night. That's what pays for the band."

"Oh, I see. Well, thanks very much," said Sara as she was twisting the cord around her fingers and then hung up. How could she justify one tenth of her grocery allotment each week to go and satisfy her curiosity. She picked up the phone again and dialed Lucy's number.

"Hey, Lucy, it's Sara. You remember that man? Well, according to that magazine picture, he plays with a group called Happy Tears. They are playing down the street tonight. There is a five-dollar cover charge, but all the drinks are free, as it's ladies' night. Would you go with me?" Sara blurted all that out in one long breath.

"Sara, you are kidding, right? I haven't been to a bar since I got married fifteen years ago."

"No, listen, Lucy. That guy has not been coming around since I went screaming down the street."

"Geez, Sara, do you blame him? He probably thought you were some crazy idiot."

"Exactly, that's what I thought. I have to get a closer look, and even though five dollars is a huge bite out of my weekly grocery money, I need to do this."

"Okay, okay. I will go for one drink and one drink only. Might even be straight drink like cola. We're going to stay long enough for you to get a looksy, and then we're out of there. Deal?" Lucy said.

"Yes, okay. Thank you. Now I've got to figure a way to tell Joseph," Sara said, pacing up and down her kitchen.

"Just tell him some of the girls in the neighborhood are going to see this new band. You will only be gone a couple of hours and you would really like to go. So what time did you want to leave?"

"How about eight thirty?" said Sara, still pacing.

"Deal. I'll drive. Be by your house around eight thirty to pick you up."

They hung up the phone, and Sara decided to start dinner. They were having beef stew tonight with dumplings. She really liked home-cooked meals for all seasons. She browned the beef cubes and then added celery, onion, carrots, and potatoes. She had it cooking on the back of the stove on low.

She went to her room, showered, and washed her hair. And then she went to her closet. All she owned these days were jeans, sweatshirts, some blouses, and a few cardigans. She wasn't there to be a fashion queen, so she chose jeans, blouse, and a cardigan. She put a few curlers in her hair and hauled out the portable hairdryer. She sat and read a magazine for a while.

"Mom, where are you?" yelled MJ.

"Mom? Yo-ho, Mom!" yelled Lacey.

She awoke with a start. She didn't even realize she was sleepy.

"In my bedroom, kids." The auto setting on her hairdryer had turned off a long time ago. The kids came in and asked her for their after-school snack. She had been so wrapped up in her own thoughts that she had forgotten.

"Be right there to fix you something," Sara said while her brain was ticking off items available.

"How about a dish of cherries or some chunky applesauce, milk and graham crackers," she asked.

Both kids said the applesauce was good, so she got down several bowls, a couple of glasses, the applesauce out of the refrigerator, and, of course, graham crackers. While they were eating, she asked them about their day, whether or not they had homework. She then told them that she was going to be gone for a while this evening with her friend, Lucy, but that their dad would be home.

Both Mark and Lacey answered their mom's questions and then said, "Have fun!"

Joseph was all for the idea, so with the go-ahead, they went.

Happy Tears was a Country-Western band in a Country-Western nightclub. Sara should've known. What other music ever written had the number of ballads that country music had? Well, the one good thing was that Sara found herself in perfect dress code for Western, except she didn't have the boots. She and Lucy found a table as close as she could get to the band.

The band came out and introduced themselves as Happy Tears and that they were there for their country pleasure. The Band played a couple of fast songs just to get the place swinging, even if it was too early for anyone to get out on the dance floor. Not enough drinks in them yet. Sara kept straining her neck to look at the guitar player. She couldn't quite see him. She started looking at each player, but she didn't see whom she was looking for.

Sara waited for a break in songs and went up to the bandleader to request a song. She asked if all the band members that had been in the magazine picture were here tonight. Why, no, he told her one of the guys who used to play with them had to drop out because of medical reasons. He told her the guy went by Johnny, and that was all he knew. The guy just showed up when he was told and left when they were done; he never hung out socially with them.

In the morning, Sara got Joseph off to work and the kids off to school, and over her cup of coffee, she decided she would get her morning housework done, and then she was going to look for the box that held Mark's old letters.

She spent the morning going as fast as she could with her housework. She found the box she was looking for, and over her sandwich, she started to go through them starting with the last letter she received.

My dear Sara,

It seems like months since I saw you last, and yet when I look at the calendar, it has only been weeks. The time went so fast when we were on R&R, and yet back here it seems to drag on and on. In another four months, I will be home with you, and another two months after that I will be out of the service for good.

In your last letter, you thought you might be pregnant. Is everything going okay? How are you feeling? Have you thought of any baby names yet?

I got a letter from your mom and your sister today. They are very nice to have for family, but apparently, you haven't told them of your pregnancy because neither one of them mentioned it to me.

I love you so very much, and I can hardly wait until I have your arms around me again.

Your hubby,
Mark

This wasn't the last letter, Sara remembered. They must be out of order. She had a huge lump in her throat, but amazingly it did not bring tears to her eyes. She put the letter in the box and searched for the last one. She ran out of time, as the kids were due home any minute, so she took the box to her room and put it under her side of the bed. She was walking down the hallway when the kids burst through the front door. She fixed them a bowl of peaches and a piece of cinnamon toast for a snack.

At four in the afternoon, she started browning the pork chops. With the help of some canned mushroom soup poured over the chops to form a gravy, dinner was near ready when Joseph walked in.

"Hey, you weren't out very late last night."

"No, a couple of the girls couldn't make it last minute, so Lucy and I went and visited over a couple of diet colas and came home."

"Well, it was good for you to get out for a while anyway. Did you have fun?" asked Joseph.

"Sure, Lucy and I had a girl talk, and that is always fun."

Dinner was done, and so were the dishes, and Sara put up their ironing board so she could iron for a bit while her TV programs were on.

Tomorrow she would put all the letters in date order. She couldn't remember what was special about the last letter, but she would remember when she found it.

# 9

He was going to have to find a job; he only had so much money left. He had gotten a paper at the store a few hours ago, and it was spread out on the table for him to take a look at.

He was too old to be a grocery bagger and too young to be a part-time Santa Claus. See, here was a job for a school janitor, and it was at the kid's school, so it was perfect. Any person having served in the armed forces had the proper training to be a janitor. He called the number and accepted an interview time for tomorrow. Perfect!

# 10

It took Sara several days working on the sly to get the letters in date order. How did they get so badly out of order? Had she been crying and just grabbed one to read and put it back out of order?

Sara set the table and stirred the sweet-and-sour pork over white rice. She had two extra pork chops that she had browned, cut up, and saved. She had added onion, green pepper, and pineapple into it, along with a packet of sweet-and-sour sauce mix. That was how she made her grocery dollar stretch.

She continued to iron a little that night when her programs were on TV because it freed her up a little in the daytime. She got the kids' stuff all pressed that night and went to bed really tired. She felt like she was running night and day at this time. She had gotten the presents wrapped in the morning after she literally ran around, made beds, picked up the dirty clothing, and started the washer. She quickly vacuumed the house and swished the toilets.

The next day, she sat down and read a few more letters from Mark.

> Dear Sara,
>
> How are you, baby? I miss you so much sometimes I can't stand it. I have to keep myself very busy so as not to think about you. We have been going out on daily missions and sweeps. I want you to know something, if I should die here in Vietnam, I want to be buried in a nonmilitary grave. You might ask why, but I will explain when I get home—alive.
>
> My buddy, Johnny, is getting asked to do all sorts of things. I am not supposed to say anything, so please keep this a secret. He had been asked to do a special mission, and they will pay him huge bucks. He is thinking about it…

That was the letter she was thinking of. First off, come to think about it, she didn't remember a buddy by the name of Johnny. Of course, it had been ten years. Secondly, was Mark trying to tell her something? Jonathan was Mark's middle name. Oh, she just wished she had the answer to this mystery going on in her life. Once again, it was time to put away everything and get busy on fixing dinner. She would take a look at it again tomorrow. She almost needed to go backward to try to rebuild what had happened the last few weeks before Mark was killed. There was something else, but she just couldn't remember.

She got busy and put on a big pot of split pea and ham soup. She got some frozen rolls out of the freezer and put them on her cookie sheet to thaw and to rise. They had not had ham recently, so she just bought a ham steak at the store and added the onion, the water, and the split peas.

About the time the rolls would need to go into the oven, the soup would be done. She sat for the next couple of hours and addressed Christmas cards. Okay, so the decorations were up, the gifts had been wrapped, they had had their open house, and now she just needed to do the Christmas cards as the last piece to get Christmas done. She would need to go grocery shopping for Christmas dinner but other than that, she was ready.

Christmas came, and they had a wonderful day. Joseph had given her a small diamond heart, and it was gorgeous. It really sparkled in the right light and made her feel like a very special lady. She had given Joseph a new watch, which he desperately needed. The kids got a couple of things off of their lists and were really happy about what they had received. Next year she would be taking knitting lessons, and so she hoped under the tree next year would be a sweater for everyone. That was a huge undertaking and only one year to make three sweaters, but she was determined.

When the kids were home, she had no time to look at letters, so she just set the project aside until they went back to school. The New Year's came, and they celebrated it at home with movies and popcorn, hot chocolate, and banging pots and pans out the front door at midnight. It was really a lot of fun.

She thought she saw Mark's car around the corner when she left to go to the grocery store one of the days the kids were home and were in the car with her. She went zooming by the car and then realized she recognized it. She turned around, but by the time she got back to where the car had been parked, it was gone. That was the first time she had seen him in months.

The school year continued on, and the kids were busy in springtime sports. It was time to start working in the yard in the evenings and get the flower beds worked up again and the vegetable garden. It was a little bit too early to actually plant but only to get the ground ready. The kids helped again with the planting of the vegetable garden. It was really a good thing that they were willing to help her and really enjoyed the vegetable garden.

MJ had his tenth birthday in June. Sara had a little party for him, inviting his school friends and some of Lacey's friends. She had the backyard all decorated and had also made sandwiches, chips, pop, and cake. She had come up with a few games that the kids could play, like old-fashioned sack races and carrying the egg on a spoon, and also had prizes if you happened to be the winner. She wanted MJ to always remember his tenth birthday. It was after all a double-digit birthday, being ten. It was a fun day for everyone who attended, and MJ had a great time. Later that day, Sara was cleaning up the yard. Joseph had gone up to Kentucky Fried

Chicken to buy them some dinner. After getting ready for the party, decorating, having the party, and cleanup, she was not willing to make dinner too.

A month later, they celebrated Lacey's birthday as she turned twelve. MJ would be in the fifth grade come September, and Lacey would be a seventh grader, middle school! Once again, MJ would get home before her. Lacey wanted a dance party. And so once again, they took all their own old forty-fives and decorated the yard with lots of music around. She invited her class, and of course MJ was allowed a few of his friends. They barbecued hot dogs and had fruit and potato salad, and for desert, they had cupcakes decorated with black licorice to form a record with a red hot candy for the center. Lacey loved everything. It was really fun to be creative and to have these special birthdays for her children.

The kids helped her once again with the garden, the canning, and in making more jam for the freezer; they were a huge help. Lacey was helping her can peaches and was too anxious to get the jars from the cold water bath over to the cooling counter. She had a pot holder around the top, but there must have been extra hot water on the lid because as she started to pick it up, the hot water soaked into the pot holder and onto her hand. She dropped the whole thing, and when it broke, hot peaches and juice splashed up on her barely covered legs. Sara had to stop what she was doing. She grabbed cold water and towel and then rushed her to the emergency room.

They treated both legs, but it was mostly one that got it the worst. They put the special cream on them and wrapped them with a light gauze. They gave her something for pain, and then Sara took her home. She hobbled downstairs and planted herself in front of the TV. It was always cooler in the basement anyway. Sara checked on her several times and found her sleeping. She had refilled the pain relief and the ointment and picked up some gauze, so she could keep her comfortable these days of healing.

MJ was beside himself. He would sit downstairs with her for hours. What could he do when his best friend and sister was hurting? He kept her company when she was awake, but when she slept, he went to help his mom. They wouldn't be going swimming for a few weeks anyway. Hopefully they would be able to by the end of summer.

Joseph was so grateful that Sara had handled the emergency so efficiently. He came home and checked his baby girl and gave her a kiss on the forehead. She was asleep, but somewhere her dreams would be safe knowing her daddy was home. He offered to barbecue hamburgers since the kitchen was such a mess from canning, and Sara appreciated that. When she had gotten home from the emergency room, she had to clean up the peach mess all over the floor. That was quite an ordeal. Nothing like cooled down peach syrup dripping from your cupboards and broken glass everywhere.

In a few days, Lacey was feeling much better. She was able to get up and move around. They kept applying the ointment for a few days following, but then they were able to keep the gauze off. It looked at first like her leg would be scarred, but not now that healing was taking place.

School started with a few new outfits for each. They both were so excited. Sara still had pears to do and had them lying out on her garage floor upon newspaper. Each day she would go out and pick up the ripe ones, prepare them for the canning jars, and process them the appropriate time.

One day, there was a knock at the front door. No one was there; however, there was a small bouquet of Sweet William, one of her favorite flowers, with a note, "I must talk to you." She looked around to see if she could see anyone up and down the street. No one.

She took the flowers into the house and put them in water. They really brightened up her kitchen. But who was this person needing to talk to her?

She fixed tacos that night for dinner, along with Spanish rice and fruit. She and Joseph worked in the yard, getting things ready for winter—digging up the annuals and tossing them into the recycle or taking the seeds from them when they were dried a bit. She also loved zinnias. And one thing that Lucy had shown her was how to take the seeds out and dry them. Then the next year, she'd make a patch of zinnias by tossing them onto the ground and then sprinkle with a light covering of dirt and water. They were always beautiful on the side of the house. Who would know that one of her favorite flowers was Sweet William? Joseph never questioned where the flowers came from but just commented how pretty they were.

# 11

He knew he was being brazen to walk up on her porch, lay the flowers and note down, ring the bell, and then run like heck. He couldn't help himself. Maybe that was his problem. Maybe he was getting too emotional about this whole thing. He had found the job at the school as a janitor. Now only the boy was at that school, while the girl was at the school next door. He could still keep his eye on both of them though. He knew if he got caught he would pay for his past sins, and that frightened him a bit. He was not entirely a free man.

He opened a can of soup and heated it on his one-burner stove. He took bread and mayo and a couple slices of cheese and made a sandwich. It was crude living this way, and he hated it. He wanted to approach the lady but was scared of what she might think or do.

# 12

The kids wanted to have a Halloween party the Saturday night before Halloween. They wanted to dunk for apples and wanted a spooky house too, so a few weeks before, they all sat at the table and made plans. They would turn the spare bedroom into the spooky house. Peeled grapes would be eyeballs, cooked spaghetti noodles would be brains, etc. That would be fun. They could play "Monster Mash" on the record player and dress in costumes.

Sara made marshmallow treat bars with candy corn mixed in and, of course, pumpkin cookies decorated like jack-o'-lanterns. She made chicken salad sandwiches and deviled eggs using sliced black olives for spider legs.

Her thought was if that was Mark who had been spying on her, he would know his loss more and more as he saw kids coming to this great party they had planned. He could see how much she loved her family and what he had missed out on. She didn't see him around right now, though, so she could think all she wanted, but if he wasn't there to witness this party, then she was just talking.

The next day was Sunday, and they had fun clearing all the Halloween stuff from the basement. It had been a pretty successful party with all the girls screaming as they went through the haunted house blindfolded. Some of the young boys acted like they wanted to scream but actually didn't. Joseph and Sara were really proud of their children. They had acquired some social graces somewhere to keep the party going and to entertain their friends. On Sunday, the phone didn't stop ringing as Lacey got phone call after phone call saying it was the most fun Halloween party they had ever been to. They said thanks for the invite!

Monday, everyone was gone—to school and to work. *Hooray*, Sara thought. She had a day to herself. She went and got Mark's letters and continued reading some of them. She remembered what she had been looking for. It was in one of his later letters. She found what she was looking for and proceeded to read it.

> Dear Sarie,
>
> I love you so much and miss you to the point of wanting to go AWOL to be home with you. And then on the other hand, they are offering large sums to extend. What would you think of me extending for six months? I know we could use the money. I know it would mean you could quit work earlier, and that would make me happy. I would do it for you. I would do anything for you. Well, think about it. They

will need my answer soon. The money would come directly to you, not to me. So much to think about. So much when I should be thinking about fighting and staying safe so I could come home to you. I will write more later. I am so tired tonight after today's mission.

Your loving husband,
Mark

She had forgotten he used to call her Sarie. It was strange at first, but then it grew on her. So he was asking her opinion on extending his time over there. Well, maybe he decided to do that, but if he did, why would the military send him home in a casket? Just too many questions and not enough answers. She kept the two letters out of the stack tied with a bow. Somehow in these two letters, he was trying to tell her something. But what exactly was it?

This year at Thanksgiving, both grandparents were invited. Sara slow-cooked the turkey in order for it to stay juicy. She made dressing with sausage, celery, onion, and raisins. It was really good. The whole meal turned out well. She decided to make homemade cranberry sauce and added orange to it. She cut up the orange into small bits, plus some of the rind, and made it taste delicious. She took refrigerator rolls out of the freezer, and they smelled homemade when baked. Lacey and MJ were always jumping around together. They were excited to see the grandparents and also of the four days off of school.

This time, she found a very small bouquet of mums on her front porch when she answered the door. No note.

This whole thing was strange. Why didn't he just come out and say something about it. By now, it had been ten years since she lost him. If it was him and he came to her door, would she fall into his arms? Would she cry and be so happy that he was alive after all? Would she leave Joseph and Lacey to go with Mark? These were questions she couldn't answer.

She made turkey noodle soup for dinner and also put together a creamy, cheesy turkey casserole for dinner the next night. She was down to the carcass after several nights of Thanksgiving leftovers. She had made zucchini bread and pumpkin bread, so she was trying to decide which one to have with the soup. Maybe she would slice up some of both.

Lucy called, "Hey, Sara, would you want to go shopping within the next couple of days. Meier and Frank are having their red tag sale, and I cut a couple of twenty percent and fifteen percent coupons to use. Do you have any extra money in the piggy bank for such a sale?"

"I think I could scrape up a few dollars." Sara joked back to Lucy.

"Good. Then I will pick you up about eleven o'clock. Lunch is my treat, and then we shop!"

"Okay, that sounds like fun. I haven't been on any kind of shopping trip except groceries for so long."

The next morning, after she got everyone out the door, she buzzed around the house to try to get some semblance of order. She took a quick shower and got dressed and was ready by eleven o'clock. She got in the car, buckled up, and said, "Let's go get 'em—sales, that is!"

They had lunch at a fast food restaurant and was shopping by twelve o'clock. Lucy said that she perused the whole store and that we would meet back by the cosmetic counter. So they went their separate ways. Sara went first to the men's department to see if she could find a couple of dress shirts for Joseph. She found exactly two in his size that would be considered a good bargain but something he could wear. She found a shirt for Lacey, a shirt for MJ, and for Lacey a real pretty little blouse. For herself, she got a new pair of jeans and two shirts—all for thirty-five dollars. She couldn't believe it. How could they stay in business like that? Lucy explained that these were the leftovers, the one-of-a-kind goods, the clearance racks.

They went home, and like usual, she had to wash and iron everything before they could be put away. How did she know how many hands had been all over those clothing items?

She was downstairs at the laundry when the doorbell rang. Sara went to answer the door. Who could be ringing her doorbell now? When she opened the door, it was the man who looked like Mark. What a surprise! Here she had been chasing this guy down for years, and here he was in front of her. She dropped what she had in her hands, as she was almost in shock.

"Are you related to Mark Williams?"

"Yes, I am."

"Who are you?"

"Sarie, it is me, it's true. Can I come in and talk to you for a few minutes, please?"

"How do I know you are Mark?"

"We walked along the waterfront after our senior prom and vowed our love for one another."

"That still doesn't mean anything. Just tell me what you want."

"I want a chance to explain what has happened. Sarie, I am alive, and I have a story to tell you."

Sara stood, and while she was crying very hard, she said to Mark, "If it is you, Mark, and you have tricked me all these years, you get out of here. I don't want to hear any of your stories or reasons of why you would do this to me and MJ. It is the cruelest thing I could ever think to do to another human being. Get out of here now!"

"But, Sarie, I need to talk to you."

"No way! I am not even going to give you the time of day. I don't want to hear your excuses." Sara went and opened up the front door. "Now you get out of here and don't come back. I don't believe you are Mark. He was a gentleman who would have never done something like this to his wife and son. I think you are an impostor, and I want you to leave my family alone. Do you hear me? Alone. Now leave!"

*How dare him. How dare him! Who does he think he is, pretending to be Mark?* She was so angry.

She went into the house and called Lucy. "Lucy, this is Sara. Can I come down for a few minutes? The most horrible thing just happened to me."

"Of course you can, Sara. You are always welcome," said Lucy, wondering what she was in for.

"I will be right down then."

She got down to Lucy's house and knocked on the front door. She heard a "Come on in," and she did. As soon she saw Lucy, she started to cry.

"Sara, oh my God, what happened? I have never seen you cry. You must really be upset."

"Lucy, that man came to my house saying he was Mark. He said he was alive and that he could explain everything. But I told him to get out. I was so angry at him for making a fool out of me and pretending to be Mark. I am just so angry I don't know what to do with my anger."

"But, Sara, if you kicked him out, you won't know the reason. You don't know the why. You don't even know if that was really Mark."

"I understand that, but at the time, I was so angry with him that I couldn't see straight. I just wanted him out of my sight. Seriously, who would do that to another person?"

"Well, one thing you can do with it is set it aside. I know that's a very hard thing to do. I also think you need to sit and talk with Joseph about this whole thing. You have been keeping it a secret for far too long. You do not want to ruin your relationship with Joseph, especially when you are so angry with this guy. He has something to tell you, and he will be around again to try. But in the meantime, come clean with Joseph."

"Lucy, you're right. I know that I owe Joseph an explanation, but this whole thing is going to get way worse before it even starts to get better. Mark was the love of my life, and now if he's back, what am I to do with that?"

"Sara, you are to take life one day at a time. Joseph is in the forefront, and you need to think of his feelings about this whole thing. How would you feel if his wife suddenly came back and wanted him?"

"That would suck, Lucy. I would think that would be horrible. I would feel so insecure."

They talked for a few minutes more, and then Sara went home to face Joseph.

"Sara, what's wrong? You need to talk to me," said Joseph.

"I know, Joseph, I know you're right. Okay, so I will start at the beginning," said Sara, taking several sips from her wine glass. "Joseph, when MJ was three, we were playing at a playground, and I thought I saw Mark hiding behind a tree. When I grabbed MJ and started walking toward the man behind the tree, he suddenly was gone. This has gone on since that time. As of late, I would see him sitting in a car, and one time I ran down the street yelling and screaming at him. But he would always take off before I could get a closer look. Today when I was doing laundry, there was a knock at our front door. It was this man I had seen before. He wanted to talk to me, to set the record straight on what had happened. I got so angry with him I wouldn't listen. I just made him leave. I started shaking and crying. I was just so angry I didn't know what to do with my anger, and then that's when I went down to see Lucy. She helped me through this, but she was the one that told me I needed to come home and tell you."

"Well, my goodness, what a surprise. I thought once a person died, they were dead and gone."

"I know, Joseph, that was my understanding too, but I don't even know if this man is Mark. I wouldn't let him explain. I just told him to get out, and I don't know where to find him! Oh my God, Joseph, if it is Mark, would I still be married to him?"

"That I don't know. Maybe you could call someone and ask?" said Joseph with a smile in his voice, trying hard not to laugh. It wasn't funny, and yet it was.

"Okay, I will make a plan and try to find this man. I don't even know where to start. Geez, I don't want to go to jail for being married to two men at one time!" Sara said while socking Joseph in the arm for not taking this whole thing very seriously.

The next day, Sara got out the phone book. She first called the recruiter station. She honestly didn't know where to start, and she felt they would give her instruction where to go.

"Marine Corps recruiter station, may I help you?" said the officer answering.

"Yes, sir, my name is Sara Williams Christopher. I thought I was the widow of Mark Williams, but he came to my door the other day, and now I need information. Can you direct me?"

"Ma'am, we have never had this happen before. Are you sure he was your husband?"

"Yes, sir, I was as shocked as you are now. Seriously, this is a problem."

"Ma'am, I really don't know whom to turn this over to. Can I take your phone number and talk to my superiors and get back to you? It might take a day or two."

"Oh. Okay. I was hoping I could settle this today. But call me back as soon as you can."

"Yes, ma'am, I will. I have your phone number here, and I will call you."

Sara got off the phone feeling dejected. She was beside herself. She had taken the officer's name and marked in her notebook the date, time, and person she had talked to and the phone number.

She looked through the phone book, but she was stuck until the officer called her back. There was no one else locally to call. She did see a 1-800 number. She marked the number in her notebook. She would call if this officer did not get back to her within three days.

Sara got busy with cleaning and laundry. She hung everything outside, as it was a beautiful day. It was cold and crisp, but the sun was shining. She went around to each room, got the beds made, and picked up dirty clothes. It was amazing how much everything looked straightened with just that done and the dishes. She sat down and made out her grocery list and was clipping this week's coupons. She decided there was enough time to get to the store before the kids got home, so she left the house.

At the front door, she found a note. "What is the boy's name?" was all it said. She looked up and down the street but didn't see any strange cars. He must have come up to the door when she was hanging clothes on the line. She wrote on the bottom of the note, "Mark Jonathan Williams, Jr.," and put it back on the door.

She went off to get her groceries.

# 13

The week went by with no more notes. The original one was not picked up, but she kept it there. She and Joseph talked about it a lot. She told Joseph that the guy at the recruiter's office probably thought she was crazy, so he was just ignoring her.

In her heart now, she wished she would have had him sit down with her and Joseph and told her what had happened. But it was too late now.

The note hung on the door for weeks, and Sara was almost ready to take it down. One day, when she went out to get the mail, she found a sweet little bouquet of red roses, white mums, and evergreens. The white mums had some pretty silver glitter sprinkled all over them. There was another note. "So the boy is mine?" She answered it, "Depends on who you really are!"

She got all the Christmas stuff out of storage from the garage and started doing some decorating. It looked really nice by the time the kids got out of school. It was hard to believe another year had gone by already. It seemed like it was just a few days ago. She sat for a moment before the kids were coming home and reflected on the last year. She had been married to Joseph two years and known him for five. They had worked in the yard and had a beautiful yard; in fact, it probably was the prettiest yard in the neighborhood. It was one of the biggest yards in the neighborhood. They had grown most of their own vegetables and fruits and canned them. It was a productive year. She had been able to stay home and take care of her family, which was always a dream of hers, not because she was lazy but because of the opposite. She didn't want to buy services like a cleaning lady and fast food; she wanted to be able to do it herself. Would she trade her life now if she could? She didn't think so, even if this man turned out to be Mark, the love of her life.

That was on a Friday. And the next day, they went to get the tree. Sara put on Christmas music while they decorated the tree, and afterward they had hot chocolate and admired their decorations. Usually, they put on colored lights, and this year they had chosen to put on the small white lights. It wasn't as colorful, but the white seemed almost like snow. On Sunday, Joseph and MJ decorated the outside lights, while Lacey and Sara finished decorating the downstairs. They weren't going to have an open house this year, maybe next year. On Monday, while the kids were in school for their last week before Christmas break, Sara got all the presents wrapped. She was able to make Lacey a pink sweater and MJ a navy sweater. Other than that, that was all she had time to knit this past year. But she was proud of what she had done.

She had the kids help her with grocery shopping this year for Christmas dinner. They voted on ham and cheesy potatoes for dinner instead of turkey. Christmas was on a Thursday this year, so Joseph had the day off before for Christmas Eve, and their company decided there was no use opening up the day after Christmas for just one day, so that was a paid day off also. Five whole days with the family—this would be fun.

On Christmas morning, Joseph went out to get the paper and almost tripped over a package. A note attached said, "This is for Mark Junior." Joseph took it into the house and gave it to Sara. Sara slipped down the hall with it and put it in her closet. She would deal with that later.

They opened the gifts, and the kids loved their sweaters. Sara felt a certain amount of pride. They had a few other gifts that were also on their lists. Sara had found the items on sale, so she was able to buy a couple of little things with the money left over. For her husband, she had found a cozy bathrobe and a special book that he wanted. It was more like a coffee table book about the presidents of the United States. It had about four or five pages each president plus pictures or drawings. It was actually a very interesting book and would keep him occupied for many a winter hour. For Sara, from the kids she got new slippers and a new nightgown. From Joseph, she got a new bathrobe (great minds think alike!) and a beautiful pair of earrings that she could wear with her jeans and blouses.

They cleared up the papers, and then Sara went to put a breakfast casserole in. It was another recipe that Lucy had given her. Made with eggs, cheese, bacon and day old bread, it was yummy and easy to make plus inexpensive. That Lucy, where there was a buck to be saved, she would find the way. While breakfast was cooking in the oven, they all went to get their clothes on. When they sat down to eat, Sara surprised them all with homemade cinnamon rolls to go with the casserole plus orange juice and coffee and—ta-da!—a wonderful Christmas morning breakfast. Her goal for the upcoming year was to make more homemade bread instead of buying it at the day-old-bread store.

The phone rang, and Sara went to answer it.

"Merry Christmas, Sara speaking."

"Just who I want to talk to," said the man.

"Who is this?" Sara asked.

"You know who it is. This is Mark," said the man.

"No, it can't be. What do you want?"

"I wanted to know how Mark Junior liked his present I got for him."

"I haven't given it to him yet. I wanted to open it and see what it is. If this is Mark, he knows only a little about you. Joseph is his daddy now. You have no right barging into his life and assuming he will know who you are. When he was little, he only had a few pictures of his daddy who died in the war. That is how he knew you. How did you get this number?"

"I found it in the white pages. Merry Christmas, Sara," he said as he was crying. There was a lapse of a few seconds before he hung up the phone, and she could hear him actually bawling. He said something like, "Oh my God, what have I done?" And then it went to the dial tone.

Sara found Joseph and asked him to follow her to their bedroom. She told him about the phone call and how it ended. Now she was really getting worried that this man was either a sicko or really Mark. How could she find out for sure?

# 14

Sara had not heard anything for months from that man. Spring break was coming up, and Joseph announced that they were all going on an adventure. They were going to rent one of those little units you find at campgrounds, little houses, or cabins on a lakefront for a week. They were going to hike, fish, and cook by a barbecue unit that had an element for coffee and hot chocolate. It sounded really fun, and the family was all for it.

They left on a Saturday morning and would come home the following Saturday. It was cold, but it was beautiful. The unit they had rented had a very small bathroom attached, so at least, they didn't have to tromp across the campground for facilities. The unit they had, had a double bed on the bottom and a single on top, and then across from that bed was another single. Perfect. They took their sleeping bags, pillows, and extra blankets. There was a heater in the room on the wall and a table with four chairs to eat their meals on the paper plates and plastic silverware they had taken. It was not like the pioneers for sure, but they had to find something else to do than watch TV since there was none. They had taken a couple of games and books and made due in the evening.

"Mom, you want to play Rummikub with me?" asked MJ.

"Sure, honey. Let's get Dad and Lacey too. Come on, guys, let's play a game. It will be fun."

So they all gathered and soon were laughing and joking and having a really good time together. They took a hike the next day with a picnic lunch packed in both the kids' backpacks. She had a walking stick, which was a good thing. She had not been doing much walking recently except for around the house. The hike was beautiful. It was around fifty-five degrees and sunny, so the weather was definitely cooperating. The jackets they had started out with were soon tied around their waist. The river was beautiful. They sat down and had their lunch on a couple of logs and looked at the view.

"Joseph, you are a wonderful man for thinking of this. I really believe we needed this. I feel so refreshed! Of course, tomorrow I will be complaining of sore muscles."

"You are welcome, Sara. I knew all this Mark stuff was causing stress for all of us, and I needed to get us away from it. I had seen these cabins years ago when I was camping in a tent, but other than peeking in the window, I had never been inside one. I think it is working out well, don't you?"

"Well, that depends. If we wake up tomorrow and there is snow on the ground, or it is pouring rain, you get to do breakfast and the coffeepot," Sara said with a chuckle.

"Just be a pain in the tush then about it! I can do that. I am man, hear me roar."

"Sorry, Joseph, that statement is I am woman, hear me roar," Sara said with an outright laugh.

"I will pray for sunshine then," said Joseph with a smile on his face.

"You are getting spoiled. Having breakfast and any other meals fixed for you all the time, dishes done, laundry done. Joseph is spoiled, Joseph is spoiled," Sara chanted.

He grabbed her, and they rolled over on the dirt. Joseph started tickling her, and she was not a good person to tickle; she couldn't even get her breath when she was tickled. So Joseph let up when she started gasping for air in-between the giggles. They sat up, and suddenly, Sara pushed Joseph over. Then she leaned down and kissed this wonderful man. The love she had for Joseph was different than the love she had for Mark, but it was still a wonderful love.

They fished one day and, between the four of them, got enough trout to barbecue for dinner. Sara had wrapped potatoes in foil and pierced them so the steam would come out. She laid them on the barbecue rack and would turn them every fifteen minutes. She had also bought some corn on the cob and did the same routine of wrapping them in foil. She sent both kids down with the garbage can, which was filled to the brim. They played Uno after dinner was done and the dishes (paper plates and plastic silverware) were thrown into a garbage can. When everything was all cleaned up, it was game time. She rallied around until all four were sitting down. After a couple of hours, she pulled a trail mix out of her bag and found a paper bowl to put it in. It was good, just enough sweets in it that she kept everyone going for a while.

Sleepy eyes said it was bedtime. They all cozied up into their sleeping bags and extra blankets, and because it was so dark outside, no one even asked what time it was. They were all tired after their long hike today. This was so much fun. Sara again said to Joseph what a great idea it was.

Saturday came, and they packed up and then packed the car. The ride home was really quiet. No one wanted to go home; it had been so different from their everyday lives, and they had really worked together as a family. And they had played as a family.

When they drove up to the house, Sara noticed a new note on the front door. After they got the car unpacked, they aired out the sleeping bags and blankets on the line and put the pillows away, the dirty clothes downstairs, and the food into the kitchen. She went out to retrieve the note. When she opened it, she saw all it said was, "Then Mark Junior is my son?"

"Yes," she wrote on the note, along with his birth date. She was no longer angry with Mark, but she did feel sorry for him, for what he chose over her and the baby, must have been a humdinger. For him to pretend to be dead, that was what got her. She hung the note back up and wrote his name on the other side so he could see it was return mail.

Sara went in and put some dinner together. As she was fixing, she wondered where this was going to go. What was going to happen? So many unanswered questions.

# 15

Mark was lying on top of his bed, thinking. He had really messed things up so far. What did he think, that she would just jump into his arms? Let him sweep her away like in the storybook tales? The only thing he could hope for would be to keep asking questions with notes on her porch. After a while, she might get used to him being around. He had waited so patiently for his ten years to be up. That was part of the deal—he could contact people from his past after ten years. What did he expect, that her life would stop altogether? That she would never find companionship again? That she would never remarry?

What could he ask in his next note? He wanted to start bringing up memories. He wanted to make her remember what it was like being married to him. I know he would ask her if she still had the house they had bought together. And so that was what he did.

He always picked the time she went grocery shopping to put the note on her front porch. He got the answer back. "Yes." She still had the house, and they were using it as a rental.

Did she ever see any of their old friends? He had asked her. "Yes, a few," she answered. Mostly, she and Joseph had tried to meet new friends together.

Doggone it, why did she have to bring up Joseph! He had to put more thought in how he asked these questions. At least, he got to see his son every day at school. Mark Junior's room was always the first room he did so that he could watch the kids come out of the classroom.

# 16

Sara had tried the recruiting station again to see if they had any further information for her. He gave her the name of the local chaplain and said he might be able to help. Sara contacted him to tell him her story, and he said he would find out and give her a call back. He tried to talk to her about grief, about seeing people that looked like the lost loved one. She assured him it was him. She had even been writing notes back and forth to him.

The chaplain asked why she wanted help from the military when she had contact with him. She said she wanted to know why the government had chosen to make a fool out of her. Why did they pretend he was dead when he wasn't? What was the deal? The chaplain explained that unfortunately, if it was, by chance, a covert operation, they would not give her any details whatsoever. Her husband—or her first husband—must have had a good reason for doing what he did. He had been supposedly dead for how long, the chaplain wanted to know, probably over ten years now. He said he would get back to her when he had something, and in the meantime, he would say a prayer for her.

Great, he would say a prayer for her. She wasn't yet ready to face Mark. This note writing was okay for now because she just couldn't be put on the spot between Mark and Joseph—she just couldn't. Someday she would be ready and would invite him into her home to explain, but if she could get a hint of what was going on through the government, that would suffice her for a while.

Sara got busy with the laundry, and then she sat down and knitted for a while. Next winter, she was planning on taking a Stretch and Sew class. She would learn how to make casual shirts for Joseph and knit pants, skirts, and tops for Lacey and herself and T-shirts for MJ. That would also be fun, but for right now, spring and summer, it was knitting.

She got a snack ready for the kids, and then she hung the clothes up outside and started dinner. Tonight they were having tacos, refried beans, and corn. Sara loved tacos. In fact, she could eat Mexican food six days a week, but the family wouldn't let her. Next week, she was going to fix enchiladas with green sauce. She took cooked chicken, black beans, and cheese. Then she rolled up the enchiladas and put them into a pan. She spread the green sauce all over them and then topped them with cheese before serving them with sour cream. *Oh my gosh*, she thought. *I have to stop thinking about them because my mouth is salivating*.

The kids came bouncing in the door right about then.

"Hey, Mom, what's for snack?" asked Lacey. "I am starving."

"Mom, what is for snack? I beat Lacey from the bus stop, I should be able to ask first!" said MJ.

"Don't get too excited. I decided to make you chocolate pudding with lady finger cookies. I think you are supposed to make it with vanilla, so let me know how it tastes, will you?" said Sara.

"Yum, this is good! I really like it," said MJ.

"It's okay, but I think I would like to try it with Vanilla next time. I think the cookies are supposed to melt or something into the pudding. I read that somewhere. Don't know where though," said Lacey.

"Hey, Mom, we got a new janitor at school, and he is really nice. I guess he has been there for a while, but I just now noticed 'cause he's always waiting for our classroom to empty so he can get started on the cleaning. He always smiles at me and tips his hat, like this," said MJ.

"That's really nice. Does he do that to any of the other kids or just you?" asked Sara.

"He does it to lots of the kids. That's what makes him so nice."

"Well, catch me up on what else is new, kids."

"I like a boy at school, Mom," said Lacey rather shyly as she looked down at her pudding, twirling the same spoonful over and over.

"Well, that is big news. Tell me about him."

"He is taller than me, dark hair and blue eyes. His name is Tommy, and I think he likes me too. He wants to talk to me all the time before class and after too. Sometimes he walks me to the next class, and then he has to run like heck to his own class," said Lacey, blushing.

"Yes, it does sound like he likes you a lot."

"Oh, brother, all this girl-boy mushy stuff. I am outta here," said MJ, putting his dish in the sink.

"Well, anything I can do to help you, you let me know," said Sara.

"Actually, he asked me for my phone number, so he might be calling here," said Lacey.

"Then that is fine, Lacey. You will soon be going on to eighth grade, and more and more boys will be calling you because you are beautiful inside and out."

"Oh, Mom, I love you. Please don't ever leave us. I don't know what I would do if you ever decided we couldn't be a family again."

"Lacey, where did you ever hear such a thing? I don't plan on leaving anywhere."

"Mom, I heard you and Dad talking one night about some guy that was coming around, leaving you notes. I was on my way to the kitchen for water, so I didn't hear much, just that," said Lacey.

"Well, honey, I don't want you to worry about anything at all, okay?"

"Okay, I won't."

Lacey took her homework downstairs, along with MJ, and got to work on it. Sara went down to hang more clothes on the line and to take down the ones that were dry and ready to iron. She set up the ironing board upstairs and got to work. Since dinner was going to be pretty easy tonight, it was a good time to get the ironing done. She had already shredded the lettuce and cut up the tomatoes this morning.

Joseph came home while she was finishing up. "Here's another note from the front porch," he said, rather like he was irritated.

The note read, "What type of sports does MJ like? Is he going out for anything this spring?" Well, that was an easy one to answer. "MJ likes football and will sit for hours with his dad, Joseph, and watch all day on Sundays. No, he is not going out for any sports. He likes to help me plant in my vegetable garden."

That ought to fry his cookies—calling Joseph his dad. Well, he was, he was more a dad than Mark ever was. He had been around the last five years of MJ's life. In fact, he was the only dad that MJ had ever known. *Well, too bad*, thought Sara.

She thought back about all the lonely nights that she would sit for hours and cry. Think about Mark, how much she loved him and how much she was going to miss him now that he was no longer in her life. And when MJ was born, she cried all over again for the father Mark would never be and for MJ the father he would never know. She had shed a lot of tears over the years. Over and over again. She was so angry. She really didn't even know what to do with this anger.

The next day, she called the chaplain again. She asked if he was local and if she could she come and see him. They made an appointment for two days from now.

# 17

Sara drove down to the vets' hospital and walked the corridors searching for the correct room; she finally found it. It was a good thing she left early because now she was on time. She opened the door, and there was a military secretary outside the door to his office. He came out after his secretary had beeped a buzzer, letting him know his next appointment was here.

Sara introduced herself and shook his hand. She had dressed in a skirt and blouse with a cardigan today. She wanted to look a little more professional than jeans would have offered. The chaplain invited her to sit down and pointed to a chair directly across from his desk.

"Now, Mrs. Christopher, please start from the beginning," he said, getting his pad of paper and pen ready to take notes when he needed.

"My husband, Mark J. Williams, was killed February 1, 1968. I was four months pregnant when he was killed. I waited one week from the time I was notified for the body to come home. I was able to see Mark the night before the funeral at a private showing, and then the day of the funeral was open casket. Lots of people came to his funeral, lots of flowers and lots of visitors to my mother's house afterward for a reception. I was able to watch them put the coffin into the ground. I cried and cried. Mark was my world. He was my everything. We had planned so much for our future, for our baby.

"When MJ, named after Mark my husband, was three years old, I first saw a person whom I thought looked like Mark. We were at a playground about two blocks from our house. The man was standing by a tree, or rather behind the tree. I turned to grab MJ and started to walk toward that tree. The man disappeared, and I could not find him.

"Then when I got married to Joseph after having been a widow for eight years, the man showed up in Reno where we were having a short honeymoon. That was over two years ago. Then he started parking his car close by, and when I would start to approach him, he would start his car and drive away like crazy. One day, there was a knock on my front door. When I went to answer it, there was this man there that had been spying on us. He said his name was Mark and that he wanted to explain things to me. I told him if he really was Mark to get out and never come back. I was so angry with him.

"Now I get little notes on my front door—questions, really. He wants to know things, like if MJ is his son, when he was born, what his favorite sport is, things like that. I don't know what to do, how to handle all of this. It is overwhelming, and people in the military think I am crazy because all of Mark's records are marked KIA. Help me if you can." Sara was breathless when she finished. She held her hands in her lap, and they were limp, like she was exhausted already, even though this was only just starting.

"Mrs. Christopher, did you bring any of these notes with you as proof?"

"No. He would ask a question, and I would answer it and then hang it back on the door for him to take. Same piece of paper always," said Sara.

"That is a shame. Next time, take a picture of the paper or keep it and bring it in with you."

"Okay, I can do that, but in the meantime, if you believe me at all, how do I handle this? I have a nice family with Joseph and his daughter, Lacey. We all get along great, and I don't want anything to cause this family to break up. But on the other hand, I loved Mark so much. He had a great personality, he played his guitar and sang to me all the time, he loved to dance, he was frugal, and he wanted to go far in his lifetime. He wanted to go to college when he got home from Vietnam. I worked as long as I could and put as much as I possibly could into savings just so we would be a little ahead. Chaplain, his body was encased in glass. I understand that was to keep the odor contained, as most of these soldiers were dead by seven to sixteen days before burial. In Mark's case, it was sixteen days. His face was all puffy. He didn't look much like himself but enough that I knew it was him. There was no doubt in my mind."

"The military, if they did plan some operation involving your husband, would never own up to it. You have to know that. They wouldn't even tell me, and that's a fact. I guess I could continue to talk you through this experience, even though you are not a widow anymore. But other than that, I honestly don't know what I can do to help you."

"He wanted to talk to me that day. Should I have let him? I just don't know. I'm just so angry still. I'm not sure I could listen."

"I think that's up to you. I wouldn't talk to him unless you're ready to hear what he has to say. You may not like it."

Sara made an appointment with his secretary for two weeks out. She still wasn't sure what she wanted to do, but she was, at least, willing to wait for now.

# 18

Mark had been tossing and turning all night. He had dreams of the covert operation that he had performed. It brought him nightmares more often than not. He would wake up all sweaty with tears coming down his cheeks. What he had done, was it really worth giving up Sara and the baby? Was it really worth receiving the money?

The thing is, when it was presented to him, he thought it would be a great deal. The amount they were giving him was a great deal of money for 1968. Heck, it was a great deal of money still in 1978. It had been growing ever since they put it into his account. All these years, he had worked at many different jobs just to keep going, stay alive until the time he could legally talk to Sara. No one prepared him for the shock he would cause in her life. He needed to talk to someone, but who?

He attended a PTSD (post-traumatic stress disorder) group. He went by Jonathan Williams or M. Jonathan

Williams. He didn't want people to call him Mark. Most people ended up calling him Johnny. He remembered sending that one letter to Sara where he tried to warn her a little that his buddy, Johnny, was going on a special mission for the military. If he had been caught writing that to her, he would have been dishonorably discharged. He was selfish, he guessed. He wanted the money for Sara and their baby. How did he know she wouldn't end up waiting? But why should he have expected her to wait? For ten years? That was an impossibly long time he learned when one is waiting to expose himself. At the time, it seemed like it would be just a few months.

He didn't know what a production it was going to be. It was all he could do not to call it off when Sara came to see him when he was in the casket. He heard her muffled voice through the glass encasement, and he himself wanted to cry for breaking her heart. Now once again, he was sorry for breaking her heart all over again. In reality, he wanted his wife and his son back. He wanted to live in the little house they had bought together and get on with his life. He was tired of waiting. He wanted a do-over, another chance. Did he really think that Sara would leave Joseph after starting a new life with him? He didn't know the answer, and possibly neither did she.

# 19

Sara didn't hear from Mark over the next two weeks with a note on her front door. In fact, it had been months, and she hadn't heard from him. She had long ago canceled her appointment with the chaplain; if she didn't have evidence, there was no reason to keep it. She actually became worried about him but decided he would contact her when he was ready to. Maybe he was thinking about things too.

The kids helped her get her garden in, and she helped Joseph on weekends get the yard ready for another round of bark dust. Joseph was trimming bushes, the kids were picking up the pieces and putting them in the barrel for yard debris, and Sara was pulling weeds and fluffing the ground. In some areas, the bark dust was still thick, but in some areas, it was like it was washed away.

On Sunday, they all went out to breakfast. What a treat. The restaurant down the street had big, thick waffles with fresh strawberries and ice cream. It was wonderful. It was a good thing she didn't eat like that all the time, or she would be as big as a house. They stopped at the local hardware store chain and picked up geraniums in all colors—red, white, and pink—some of the Martha Washington variety. When they went home in the afternoon, they took an hour and planted them.

On Monday, Sara ordered the bark dust, and the following weekend, the entire family worked hard to get it spread. Lacey shoveled from the pile, MJ brought the wheelbarrow, and Joseph and Sara spread it. Sara would find a weed or two that had popped up and would take care of that ahead of Joseph. Lacey and MJ went in and made sandwiches at lunch, and for dinner, they had HOT-N-READY pizza. It was very good. They were all starved, as they had worked very hard all day.

Sara planted her pots for the decks the next day. They had blue Lobelia, white Lobelia, and red and pink geraniums, while some had yellow marigold and blue Lobelia; both were beautiful. They added quite a bit of color to the deck.

The phone rang just as she was pushing the final dirt into the pot. She ran to catch it while wiping her hands on her T-shirt.

"Hello," she answered.

"Hello, Mrs. Christopher. This is the chaplain. I wanted to pass on something to you that I have learned recently regarding Mark. I checked the registration for any PTSD groups at the vet hospital, and I have found an M. Jonathan Williams. Could that be him? They said he goes by Johnny."

"Yes, it definitely could be Mark. Funny in his last letter he commented about his buddy, Johnny, taking on a special mission. I thought it was really weird because I had never heard him talk about a buddy by the name of Johnny."

"He has been attending the class that meets here in the daytime on Tuesdays at twelve o'clock. You will need to bring a sandwich if you plan on attending."

"Thank you, chaplain. I just might see if I can get over my anger a little bit."

"Good luck, Mrs. Christopher. Let me know if I can be of further service to you."

"Thanks again, chaplain, really. I do appreciate it."

With that, Sara got off the phone. This was Monday, and tomorrow he would have group. Would it be so wrong for her to attend just as an observer? Well, she would give it a try.

The next day, Tuesday, she found herself again driving down to the veterans' hospital. She was looking for a certain room and finally found it. It had bleacher seating inside, and she chose the top row close to the wall. She wanted to observe but not draw attention to herself. Mark came in and took a seat about halfway up on the aisle. He never even turned around to see who was behind him. *I thought he had PTSD*, thought Sara. *Usually, these guys want to know what's around them so they can feel more confident. Hmm.*

Mark did turn just then and looked behind him and around the room. He spotted her right off, and she tried to scrunch down out of view. He stood and went to sit beside her.

"What are you doing here?" he asked her.

"I came to observe," answered Sara.

"Why? Who are you observing? Me?"

"Yes, as a matter of fact. I couldn't figure out why you would be attending a group therapy on PTSD. What did you ever do to create PTSD?"

"Well, I went through Vietnam. That would be number one. And the other, I'm not yet ready to talk about. I thought I was, but I'm not."

"So what do you do in these meetings? Just sit and listen?"

"Yes, as a matter of fact, I do. They give advice on how to get beyond the PTSD, how to wake up normal instead of in a nightmare, sweating. It's good for me to hear about others. You are welcome to stay if you want."

"Yes, I think I will."

The counselor came in the room and requested silence. Then he asked for volunteers to talk about their week. Several raised their hands, and one by one he talked with them. One guy was so angry at his wife for not recognizing that he had a problem. She was totally in denial and just could hardly take it anymore. He wanted to bring her here, but she just laughed at him. He wanted to walk away from her and the marriage. He wanted help, but he also wanted her support. The counselor advised him to sit down one more time and talk with her seriously.

"Tell her what you had just told the rest of us. Ask her to group. Tell her it is really serious and tell her that you are not threatening her in any way but that if she can't support you, you might need to separate for a while until you can get your life back together. Tell her how much you love her, and tell her how much you need her," the counselor said.

The next man said he had another unconscious nightmare, that he woke up sitting on top of his wife, and that he had punched her in the face. When she woke him up by screaming his name over and over, he felt so bad. He wanted to know how he could stop. He didn't want to hit her or hurt her; he loved her so much. "Please help me," was his plea. The counselor said he wanted to see him in his office for a private session as soon as this one was over. He thought there were some things they could do, but it was going to take practice with him and his wife. "When your wife finds herself in a compromising situation, I want her to ring a bell. I want her to ring it until you stop. You, however, will have to associate that bell with you doing something wrong. We will work on that after class," the counselor told him. "Any others?"

"My name is Johnny, and ten years ago, I did a special mission for the US government. I can legally talk about it now, but I'm not yet ready to. I had to pretend to be KIA in order to complete this mission without anyone knowing. They offered me quite a bit of cash to do this operation, and in my own selfishness, I accepted, not even thinking about the people back home, how they would take it. All I thought about was that in ten years, I would be able to start spending the money and pick up where I left off. This has not happened. In the first place, how do I get beyond the hurt that I have caused other people? That is what I'm asking today."

"Johnny speaks. Wow. This is your first time in group opening up, and what a tale you have to tell us. Well, Johnny, I guess you would want to first sit down and tell your wife how sorry you are for hurting her. It was never your intention. You weren't thinking straight because of the money involved. You probably thought you could die anyway, and so if you were already dead, so be it."

"Well, it's not that easy. I can't even get this woman to talk to me yet. I can't even get her to believe I am her past husband. She has a new family, and she doesn't even want to believe I'm alive. How can I get her to listen?"

"Johnny, you have a problem. I will need to talk to you in private. Can you please call my secretary and make an appointment? I think from here on out, you will need private counseling."

"Okay," said Johnny.

The leader called the session over for the day.

Johnny stood and shook Sara's hand. "Be seeing you around," he said to her and then left. Sara felt like she had just lost a friend, and the tears flowed all over again. She walked out to her car and sat for a long time, thinking about Johnny and what he had said about their future welfare.

# 20

The school year ended, and soon it was going to be summer all over again. Lacey and MJ went to the swimming pool every day they could, preparing jam and canning in the morning, swimming in the afternoon, and barbecuing hotdogs and working in the yard in the evenings. They really had a good time as a family, like when they got into a water fight while working out in the yard. MJ started squirting Sara, and then Sara grabbed the hose and started squirting Joseph, who then got the hose away from her and squirted Lacey. Pretty soon, they were all soaking wet and rolling on the grass, laughing. Other families couldn't figure out why Sara and Joseph's children liked to work outside with them, but if you watched them, there was a lot of love and hugging, and even laughing. It was unusual for sure, especially in this day and age, but then the answer was simple. They really enjoyed each other, and that was the true secret.

It was hard to believe that Lacey would be in the eighth grade this coming year. She would graduate at the end of the year, and MJ would be in the sixth grade.

One afternoon, when they got back from swimming, there was a note on the front door. "Can I talk to just you?"

This frightened Sara. As long as the notes had stopped, as long as she could deny that Johnny or Mark was alive, she could just deny the whole thing. She could pretend he was still dead—dead and buried up on the hill.

She answered back that she would only give him ten minutes, so he must make his best case in ten minutes.

The next note asked, "When?" She replied, "Friday at 1:00."

Friday came, and one o'clock arrived. There was a knock on the door, and Sara answered with a timer in her hands. She invited him to sit down and then set the timer.

"In Vietnam, they swore me to secrecy and then approached me to do a covert operation, which I'm not willing to talk about today. They offered me five million dollars to do this. They said that any monies you received for my 'death' such as insurance, widow's pension, Mark Junior's monies, all of it would be written off and not expected to be repaid. In my thinking, I thought ten years would go by fast. All I could think of was the money and how well I would be able to take care of you for the rest of my life. The money has been banked and has grown over the years."

"Am I still legally married to you?" asked Sara.

"No. A silent divorce was filed."

"Do you know how badly you hurt me? You chose money over me. Was I such a bad wife? Why did you hate me so?"

"That is the problem, Sarie. I love you. I still do when I know I shouldn't, as you have found happiness with someone else. I never meant to trade you in for money. I know that is what is seems like, but at the time, all I could think of was providing for our future."

Right then, the dinger dinged on the timer. "Wait, wait. There is more I want to tell you."

"Well, I suggest you make notes for next time. Give me a call in a few weeks, and I might be ready to talk again. You hurt me badly. I have to absorb this over time. It's not going to be you walk in here once and everything is just going to be hunky-dory. It will not be that easy for me, I'm sorry. No, wait, what am I telling you sorry for! Okay, Johnny boy, time for you to leave!"

"But...but...," said Johnny.

"No buts about it."

The kids had gone swimming with Lucy's kids that afternoon. They rarely went someplace with another family, but Sara knew she would need some time today, so it was Lucy to the rescue. She went into her bedroom and pulled out her and Mark's wedding picture. They looked so happy, so glad to be married. She was so proud of him and his accomplishments in the Marines. He had achieved sharpshooter marksmanship and was fast becoming a sergeant. He obeyed orders he didn't agree with and never ever gave any type of attitude. Maybe that was why they chose him.

She started to cry and cry. It wasn't that she was unhappy with what she had now; it was that she missed what she had then. She heard the kids come bursting through the door, along with Lucy.

"Hey, Sara, are you home?" asked Lucy.

"I'm in here. Be just a minute, kiddo," answered Sara. "How did the swimming go?"

"Great, those little guppies just swam and swam."

"I think I will make popcorn and lemonade for them and send them downstairs. Then you and I can talk." She opened a bag for the microwave and got out a big bowl and a pitcher for the lemonade. Then she got out the frozen concentrate from the freezer, while Lucy took out six glasses, put ice in all six, and then refilled the ice trays. With popcorn done and buttered and four lemonade glasses on the tray, they tromped downstairs to deliver the goods. Sara told Lacey and MJ that she and Lucy would be on the front porch in the shade visiting.

When they got settled on the wicker furniture, Lucy asked, "How did it go, Sara?"

"I gave him ten minutes, and I even set the baking timer." Sara chuckled. "He proceeded to tell me that he still loved me and that he never meant to hurt me and that he did it for our future. Whatever he did, they paid him five million smacks to do it."

"Oh my gosh, Sara, you are kidding me. Five million dollars is a lot of money. I wonder what he did."

"You know, Lucy, the thing that gets me is that I really, really loved the guy. I felt we would be married forever. I know forever is a long time, but I really felt that way. That is why it took me years to start dating. I knew no one would ever match up to him."

"I know, Sara, I'm sorry. I'll bet you feel like your balloon has been burst at the parade!"

"Yes, as a matter of fact, I do. Not only my balloon burst, but my gut also got kicked. I can't get beyond the hurt. It seemed like he was doing it to do the right thing, to provide for us, but on the other hand, I feel like I had been traded."

"What do you mean traded, Sara?"

"I mean some guy said to him one day, 'Here if you go do this for me, I will trade you your wife for five mil. You have to be dead, you cannot contact anyone for ten years, and by the way, you are no longer married to her.' I just feel like I got cheated out of each of those ten years!"

"I'm glad I'm not in your shoes, honey. I mean really those are tough shoes about now. I honestly hope you can get past some of this. You and Joseph are so well suited for each other and so happy."

"I told Johnny boy to give me a call in a few weeks. I think the next time, I want Joseph here. The kids might need to have an overnight adventure at their grandparents' house."

Just then all four kids burst through the front screen door. Lucy's kids were itching and wanted to go home and take their showers—so much for chlorine in the water. Lucy and her kids got into their car and drove it on up the street a few houses. She waved out the window as she drove. Sara picked up the glasses from the front porch and went in to put them in the sink. She had the kids bring up the mess from the family room, and then she loaded the dishwasher.

She got out the fixings for dinner, ham sandwiches, fruit, chips, and lemonade. They would have a picnic in the backyard. Joseph came home from work and changed into his shorts. As they were sitting down to eat at the picnic table, Sara asked Joseph if she could have a dinner date the next night, Saturday. She wanted to just spend some time alone with him. "Sorry, kids," she said. "Every once in a while, Mom and Dad have to have time alone for romance."

"Yuck," said MJ. "All that mushy stuff!" They all laughed and decided to take a walk after dinner, as it was such a beautiful evening. They ended up walking about six blocks away down to the corner drugstore that sold ice cream cones. Good thing Joseph had brought his wallet with him. They each made the walk home licking away at their cones. What a beautiful evening!

# 21

Joseph let out a whistle when Sara walked down the hall toward him. Her electric blue sheath that pulled over to one side with her reddish brown hair looked absolutely gorgeous. She had her hair pulled up on one side with a gold and blue barrette of some kind. She looked hot and sexy.

They got into the car and drove across town to Hansen's Steakhouse. At their table, they ordered a bottle of wine and a rib eye steak, which came with baked potato and vegetables. The waiter poured their wine and brought over a veggie tray and their salads and bread.

"So what's going on, Sara? Why the evening out?" asked Joseph.

"Well, I saw Mark—or Johnny, as he is calling himself. He called me and asked if he could come over and talk to me. I arranged with Lucy to take the kids, so they don't know anything about this," said Sara as she took a couple sips of wine.

"What did he have to say? And how long did he stay?" asked Joseph.

"First of all, I told him he was on the timer for ten minutes," said Sara, and Joseph chuckled. He could just picture this guy trying to outtalk a timer. "Then he proceeded to tell me that he did it for us, for our future. He said he still loved me and didn't mean to hurt me."

"Did he say what he did?" asked Joseph.

"He said he was not yet ready to talk about it. He said that they gave him five million dollars to do whatever it was and that it has been growing in a bank ever since. He works and lives off what he earns, so he doesn't touch it. It was for our future, he said. He wanted to tell me more, but the timer dinged, and he had to stop. I made him. I escorted him to the door and told him to call me in a few weeks, and we would set up a new time for him to come over. I would like to send the kids to grandparents' houses and have you be there next time. It would make me feel more secure."

"Did he say if you were still married?"

"He said no, that there had been a silent divorce. He said him being dead was part of the deal. Otherwise, it would not be believable. That is basically all the information I would let him say. That is more than what I really wanted to deal with."

"Okay, so when do you want to do this next talk?"

"I need about three or four weeks. I've got to process this, Joseph. I love you, and I love our family. We have a good thing going, and I don't want anything to jeopardize this. I want you to understand that just because he is back doesn't mean I am willing to throw everything aside."

"Thank you, Sara. That means a great deal to me," said Joseph as he took Sara's hand into his. He took his other hand and wiped a tear from his eye. "I thought because you wanted tonight to be alone you were going to let me know you were leaving me."

"Oh, Joseph, no, I would never do that. When we said I do for richer or poorer, for better or worse, through sickness and health, I meant it!"

The rest of the evening, they talked about the kids and his work and held hands. When they got home, the kids weren't there, and they took advantage of the alone time. Joseph felt better about everything after their talk tonight. He loved her very much, and he looked forward to spending the rest of his life with her.

The kids returned the next day and wanted to know how the date went. "Oh, it was fun," they both said. They decided to take a ride in the car and have a real picnic, so Sara got busy and packed a light dinner and some snacks, and then they went for a ride up to the local falls area. It was beautiful. Then they went on to the picnic area and ate.

"What do parents do on a date anyway?" asked MJ.

"Well, they talk to each other about things, have a glass of wine, a nice dinner, and go for a walk," answered Joseph.

"So no mushy stuff?" asked MJ.

"Of course, there is mushy stuff," answered Joseph. "All I can say is when you get older, you will understand."

"I am not ready for any of that mushy stuff, I will tell you what!" said MJ. "This girl at school keeps chasing me around, and she tells me that when she catches me, she is going to give me a kiss. Yuck!"

"When the time comes MJ, you will appreciate the chase." Joseph started to laugh and gave MJ a tousle of his hair. He took Sara's hand, and they both laughed together.

School started soon enough. MJ was now a sixth grader, and Lacey an eighth grader. She would graduate and move on to high school this next year. Then the boys would be calling the house! Sara had school shopping to do for each of the kids and liked to take them with her as they were getting older so they could help pick out their clothes. They each had one hundred dollars, and that was it. She suggested they check out the thrift stores to see if there was anything decent left over. MJ didn't care, but Lacey wanted all new. She was at the top of her grade now, and she wanted to look extra beautiful each day. The funny thing was when they went to the thrift stores for MJ, Lacey found some things that were brand-new and still had the original price tag on them, so that made her dollar stretch a little. They went to department stores too and shopped the sales. They wore themselves out but were able to make the one hundred dollars stretch quite far.

Johnny contacted Sara again. He wanted to know since the kids were in school again if he could come by and talk some more. Sara told him no. The only way she wanted to talk to him was in front of Joseph from now on. He asked her how she would get beyond the children being there. They would have them spend the night at the grandparents'. They set a time for two and one half weeks—Friday night at seven o'clock.

# 22

Johnny arrived at exactly seven o'clock. Sara offered him a cola or lemon lime. He took her up on the offer, and then they went out onto the deck to enjoy the Indian summer. There she introduced Joseph to Johnny. She said to Johnny, "We would like you to start from the very beginning, and we want you to be prepared to answer our questions honestly. Can you do that?"

"Yes, I will do my best," said Johnny.

"Right before I wrote that last letter to you to tell you about my friend, Johnny, being offered a special assignment for a great deal of money, they approached me to do a mission where they would have to have me pretend my death. They would pay me five million dollars, and I would have to have no contact with my family for ten years," continued Johnny.

"What was the mission?" asked Joseph.

"I'm not willing to talk about that right now, but the five million assured me that my family would not be hurting for anything in their life. It has sat in a bank, some in CDs, and has grown to five million nine hundred thousand dollars, I am proud to say. What I am not proud about is letting you think I was dead. I heard you crying while I was inside that coffin."

"And you couldn't call it off at that point?" asked Sara. "What I am having a very hard time getting over is that you traded MJ and me for money. I just can't get beyond that," said Sara.

"I didn't trade you. It was part of the deal. For everyone to believe I was not the guilty party in the mission, I needed to be dead, gone, buried, out of your life. When you were still single four and five years later, I had hopes you would wait until the ten years was up."

"Why ten years?" asked Joseph.

"That was part of the deal. The government felt that the war would be over. People would forget that the mission even occurred."

"When you saw me that day at the playground, I knew that I would have to be more careful. But you had written you were pregnant. I never got word that you had miscarried like the first time, so I assumed that the boy was mine whom you were playing with at the park," continued Johnny.

"Why did you run each time I saw you?" asked Sara.

"I wanted to be able to watch you without you knowing it. I wanted to see my son get off the school bus and walk home without him knowing it. I would never have hurt him."

"I know that, but you still spooked us for a long time. Was it you at my window years ago? I had left MJ with his grandparents, and the wind awoke me. Was it you looking in my window?" asked Sara.

"Yes, that was unfortunate. I was looking for a long time, just watching you sleep. You looked so beautiful and peaceful. The Sara I used to remember," continued Johnny. "I had to run like a son of a gun when I heard the police coming. It was the tree that had awoken you, not me. I was just looking."

"You scared me to death," said Sara.

"I didn't mean to. I honestly didn't. I was daydreaming, remembering what it was like to be curled up beside you in your lovingly warm arms," said Johnny, stealing a look at Joseph.

"Sorry, buddy," Johnny continued. "I understand she's your wife now, but at the time of the peeking, she was not married. And you guys wanted me to be honest." Johnny started to cry. "Sara, I never meant to hurt you. I love you. I know you have a new family now, and I'm the loser, but what I want to know is if there is any way we could be friends, the three of us. Can I come by sometimes and maybe meet MJ as one of your old friends, Johnny Croghan, which is my mother's maiden name?"

"Johnny, we will have to talk about it and let you know. Is there anything else you want to tell us?" asked Sara.

"Yes. I'm not planning on touching that money, and if something should happen to me, it is all yours, yours and MJ's. I want you to have it. I'm paying the worst possible price right now for this huge mistake that I made. Even the times you didn't know I was watching, I was. I worked at the playground you would take MJ to. If I saw you approaching from down the street, I would go inside the maintenance building and watch from a window. It was so worth it just to get a glimpse of you."

Sara found herself not being angry anymore but rather complimented. She knew he loved her very much, and he just confirmed it. If he didn't, he wouldn't have bothered watching all those years.

"Did you see me when I was pregnant?" asked Sara.

"That was harder because you got so you didn't walk very far. Your tummy was pretty big," said Johnny.

"Yes, it was," said Sara.

"One more question about this so-called mission you did for the government. It must have been a pretty substantial job for them to pay that amount of money," asked Joseph.

"It was," said Johnny. "And that is all I am willing to tell you about that subject. I have enough bad dreams and night sweats. That is why I am going for PTSD counseling. I just can't talk about it. I want so badly to just forget it!"

"Okay, I won't ask you again. I will wait until you are ready to talk about it. And if that doesn't come, so be it," said Joseph.

They told Johnny to wait a few weeks. They got his phone number and said they would be in touch. Joseph did ask him one more question, more on the personal side. "Johnny, I want it understood that Sara is my wife. We have a family together that works. I will not have you coming in here and making passes or flirtations with my wife, do you understand?"

"Yes, I understand. I lost out on one of the most wonderful things to ever happen in my life. If you could just allow me to be friends with Sara and MJ, that would mean so much to me. I haven't earned it, I know that, but it would mean a lot."

"Okay, as long as we understand each other," said Joseph.

"Yes, I believe we do."

Johnny left then, and Sara and Joseph went back onto the deck. They held hands while looking at the stars. It really was a beautiful night.

The kids came back and told them both what they did with each of their grandparents. MJ pulled out a sack, and there was a new sweatshirt for him and Lacey from his grandparents. It had their school's logo on it in the school colors. They were very excited about it. Sara told them she would wash them and hang them in the closets. She did put them in the washer right away with some vinegar so that the color would set. It was the only thing in the washer. Then she put them on hangers to dry. Then she took a semi cool iron to press them just a bit. That way they didn't shrink. And with growing kids, that was the worst to have their favorite items be too small for them.

She fixed chicken and dressing for dinner. She mixed onion and celery and a little chicken broth to the dressing and layered it on the bottom of the thirteen-by-nine-inch baking pan. Then she washed off the chicken breasts and patted them dry. She layered them next on top of the dressing. Then she took a can of cream of mushroom soup and spooned it over the chicken breasts. She then salted them with seasoning salt and peppered. Afterward, she put foil over the whole thing and then put it in the oven for forty minutes. You could smell it long before it was done. A green salad, some sliced oranges, and dinner was done.

After dinner, they all took a walk around the neighborhood. They decided to slowly introduce MJ into Johnny's world. The kids had asked them what they did last night, and Sara said, "We had an old friend of mine over for a little bit to visit. His name is Johnny Croghan, and I knew him before your Dad and I were married."

"Was he an old boyfriend?" MJ asked.

"We did date a time or two," answered Sara as honestly as she could.

"Dad, how did you feel about one of mom's old boyfriends coming to the house?" asked Lacey.

"Well, kiddo, a little streak of jealousy went through me for a moment or two, and then I realized I am the one married to your mom, not him!" answered Joseph.

"That's true, but it would make me jealous, I think," said Lacey. "But then I have never had a true boyfriend yet, so how would I know for sure?"

"I told your dad, and I'm telling you guys that I am not going anywhere, so, everyone, just settle down. There is to be no jealousy. Only so if I was in love with the guy still, but I don't think so," said Sara, chuckling.

They walked on and watched the trees dropping their leaves. That part was pretty, but the bare tree left behind was not. At least, it wasn't raining, and that was a very good thing. They walked on past the park and then turned around to head back. Joseph stopped Sara and put his arms around her in a very snuggly hug. "I love you, Sara Christopher. I always have from the moment I met you. I knew you were the one, and I want to live happily for the next fifty years together!"

"Fifty years. Oh my gosh, well, I had better be eating my Wheaties then! I love you too, Joseph. I really, really do."

They walked hand in hand back home, smiling at each other all the way. Sara was thinking to herself, *If I loved Mark so much, how come I can love Joseph so much? Is it because I am older? What was the deal? Now that I can have Mark back, I don't want him. I want Joseph! I want my family just the way it is.*

# 23

Halloween was just around the corner, and the discussion was on whether or not the kids were now getting too old to trick or treat. So it was decided they would have another party and invite their friends. No haunted house this time, as they had used all their old tricks before. But they would decorate with black and orange crepe paper, pumpkins, and scary things they found at the dollar store.

The kids got busy and filled out the invites and handed them out on Monday. Sara got busy with making cookies and freezing them. On Friday, the day before, she made chicken salad for sandwiches and had three different kinds of chips and a vegetable tray that she figured if no one touched she could make into vegetable soup, and punch. She also prepared orange juice, lemonade, and lemon lime drink. It wasn't too inventive, but she was still on a budget. They took her Jell-O ring mold, filled it with water, and added black plastic spiders, which were frozen and floated on top of the punch bowl.

They had a bowl of candy corn and black licorice and black jelly beans. They had set up the record player and found some music they could play. You could tell from the rumblings upstairs that they had a blast.

The kids all loved the Halloween party and talked about it for weeks at school. Both MJ and Lacey had worked together for the same goal, and Sara thought that was what made it so much fun.

They heard from Johnny, who asked if he could come by and meet the kids. She said she would talk with Joseph and call him back. They agreed he could come over, as a pretend, in the neighborhood type thing. It was to be very casual, and he could stay for one hour at the longest. They planned it for the following Friday night.

They were just finishing dinner when they heard a knock on the door. Lacey went to answer it and told Sara that an old friend of hers was here to see them. Sara went to the door and said, "Johnny, how nice to see you. What are you doing here?"

"I hope you don't mind. I was in the neighborhood and took a chance you might be home," said Johnny.

"No, I don't mind. We just finished dinner. Have you eaten? I think there's some leftover."

"No, I haven't eaten, but I wouldn't want to put you out any."

"You would actually be doing me a favor. I don't have to find small dishes to put away the leftovers. Come on in this way. Joseph, you already know Johnny. MJ and Lacey, this is my old friend Johnny Croghan that I was telling you about a month ago. Actually more than a month ago."

The kids both said, "Nice to meet you, Mr. Croghan."

"Mr. Croghan, you were our janitor last year for our classroom," said MJ.

"I was, well, how lucky was I? I wished I would have known you last year then I could have said hi," said Johnny.

"Come in and sit down. I'm sorry I don't know how warm everything is, but I will get you a plate. Here you can sit here."

Johnny sat at the table and ate the lukewarm food. It tasted absolutely delicious. He hadn't tasted food this good in years. "How is school going for you two this year?" he asked.

"Well, I love my new teacher, Mrs. Schmidt. She is so nice," said MJ.

"I have seven teachers now. I guess they are getting us ready for high school with all the class changes. Do you still work at the grade school?" asked Lacey.

"Yes, as a matter of fact, I do. They asked me if I would move to the middle school next year, and I said yes, I would. It means more classrooms but longer hours, which would mean a bigger paycheck. And I could use that, that's for sure," answered Johnny.

"Where do you live Mr. Croghan?" asked MJ.

"I rent one room from a big house on Madison at Forty-second. I have enough room for my bed, a chair to read in, a small one-person table to eat at, a one-burner element on top of my dresser, and a small refrigerator. It is not pretty, let me tell you. I'm hoping to get an apartment, even a studio apartment would be better than what I have. At least, it would have a small kitchen. I have been looking, and so far I can't find any available. If any of you hear of one, let me know."

"That doesn't sound too much fun, Mr. Croghan. Too bad Mom and Dad won't rent you the room downstairs," said MJ.

Sara chimed in, "Honey, Mr. Croghan, I am sure, would like his privacy a bit more than that. And I don't think we want to rent it out. Right now it doesn't even have a bed. And what would I do with all my sewing and knitting stuff?"

"Thanks anyway, Sara. I'll find what I'm looking for eventually," said Johnny.

Sara served ice cream for dessert with a plate of homemade cookies. They visited some more, and then the kids got busy and did the dishes for Sara since she had company. Being a Friday night, they were able to hold off on homework for tonight.

Johnny thanked Sara for the meal and said good-bye to Joseph and the children. He said he might see them around school, and if so, they were to say hello. He said it was really nice to meet the children and got in his car, waved, and drove off. Sara blew out a breath when he left only because it had gone better than she expected. Her kids were absolutely the best. They were so polite with him and remembered their manners. She was very proud of them. They went into the living room to plan for Thanksgiving. Lacey wanted to know if they would want to invite Johnny for dinner. If he was eating so poorly, wouldn't he really appreciate a good home-cooked meal? Joseph said they would think about it. They wanted to know if they should invite the grandparents this year, and both kids said a big yes!

Sara got on the phone the next day and invited both sets of grandparents. She wanted to go and talk with her mom and dad and asked if she could come by that afternoon. Of course, they said they would be home.

"I have something I need to talk to you both about. You probably won't believe it at first, but then when you hear the whole story, you will," said Sara. She repeated the story from the very beginning, the sightings through the years, and then the knock on her door explaining who this anonymous stranger was in her life. Her parents both had their mouths wide open. They couldn't believe it. She told them Joseph's parents knew nothing of this, so she would like to keep it that way. The kids wanted to invite him for Thanksgiving. She and Joseph agreed that would be a good thing to do. They thought that because of his current living conditions, he probably had no way of cooking a turkey. She knew that if they were there, they would question him, and Sara told her parents how she had met him—that she had dated him before marrying MJ's dad, which was true, just not the whole truth. It was hard to keep it from the kids, but it was necessary. Both of her parents finally agreed upon the new plan. She said he was using his middle name of Johnny and his mother's maiden name of Croghan. That way the kids couldn't trace it back to Mark Williams. Sara sat and answered all their questions, and when she left, she felt satisfied that they were all up-to-date.

Thanksgiving came, and the turkey was in the oven, which smelled heavenly. Johnny was at the door at the exact time he was supposed to be with autumn flowers in his hand and a couple of bottles of sparkling cider nonalcoholic drink for everyone. He wore khaki slacks and a wool shirt with a white T-shirt underneath. He looked very nice all cleaned up. Sara's parents were the next to arrive. The door bell rang, and Johnny went to answer it because Sara was in the kitchen checking on the turkey, while Joseph was peeling potatoes.

"Hello, Mr. and Mrs. Perkins, it is so nice to see you again. It's been a few years, hasn't it?" Johnny took his hands and patted his own widening waistline.

"Oh my god, Mar…Johnny, it is good to see you again also," said Mrs. Perkins.

"Johnny, nice seeing you, boy. I mean, you aren't a boy anymore, a man. Oh my gosh," said Mr. Perkins.

"That's okay, guys, I know it is a surprise to see me. I so appreciate Sara inviting me for dinner. I could really use a home-cooked meal. I think I'm gaining weight eating all those prepared foods from cans. All I have is a one-burner cooktop at my apartment. I'm determined I'll be in an apartment by Christmas."

After that, Mr. and Mrs. Christopher, Joseph's parents, arrived and were introduced to an old, old friend of Sara's from high school. They all sat in the living room, visiting and getting caught up in each other's lives. Soon dinner was ready, and they sat down at the table. Joseph said a blessing, which included the finding of Sara's old friend and longevity to both sets of parents. They had a great time visiting and laughing and eating way too much. They had the football game on downstairs and after everyone, including all the men, helped put away the food and did the dishes, everyone went downstairs. Sara had a table set up with desserts on them. The whipped cream and ice cream were in the extra refrigerator in the family room. She had previously set up the table with plates and forks and pie cutters. Johnny thought that was always one thing he had loved about Sara—the fact that she was always, always so organized.

Too soon for anyone's liking, the day was over. The celebration and the football games were done, and it was time to go home. Sara and Joseph loaded up plates of leftovers for them to take home, even Johnny. He was so grateful for such a wonderful meal and now leftovers. He couldn't be happier. He jokingly said, "See you at Christmas," when he thanked them for everything and was leaving.

Joseph told Sara to go peruse through the paper for her Black Friday bargains, and he would do the final cleanup. Sara had made Joseph a sweater and Lacey a shirt and a cardigan sweater. She still had to sew it all together and add the buttons, but otherwise, it was finished. She had made a couple of T-shirts for MJ, but she was looking for some fillers. They both wanted the next book in the series they were reading, needed socks, stuff like that. Because Joseph was home the next day, he was able to watch over the children while Sara went it alone. She found what she was looking for and really had not spent much money, but she was exhausted when she got home. Joseph gave her a foot rub, and she conked out for a while. They decided they wanted hot turkey sandwiches for dinner, which was an easy thing to do. When Sara awoke from her nap, she found dinner was ready. *Wow. Joseph, you surprise me*, she thought.

They enjoyed their meal and laughed and talked. She shared some of her experiences of the day, people pushing and shoving to get to the goods. The next day, they put up the outdoor lights and all the decorations except for the tree. They had found a small artificial tree at a neighborhood garage sale for a couple of dollars. They decorated it and put it downstairs on the table, so while they were in the family room, they would have a tree. Sara had picked up some white sparkly cotton at the dollar store and put that around the base. It lay flat and looked pretty good. They didn't have to buy any lights and ornaments since they had extras when they combined two households.

The following weekend, they got their tree up. It was tall and beautiful. Sara had been baking most of the week. She made several apple pies for the freezer and sugar cookies that she decorated with frosting. There were green Christmas trees with ornaments on them. There were angels, snowmen, and, of course, Santa Claus. She taught the kids how to use the icing tubes that she had, and they helped her decorate them. Then they were frozen on a cookie sheet and put into a bag and sealed. Sara also made these wonderful cookie bars that had a crust on the bottom, a filling of brown sugar and eggs, and orange juice topping; they melt in your mouth. Sara decided she would make pumpkin pies the day before Christmas.

She made a ham for Christmas with cheesy potatoes and her special yam dish. The bottom was like a custard with coconut, and the topping was pineapple and maraschino cherries. It sounded weird, but it was very delish.

Joseph and Sara debated whether to invite Johnny or not. At the last minute, they decided they would. He arrived in time for dinner, but he had packages in his arms. How sweet. They would open them when they had finished dinner and dishes.

Johnny said to Joseph, "You are a lucky man to have Sara as a cook. If I had been smart enough, I would have grabbed her when I had the chance." Sara responded, "Now, boys, no fighting!"

Joseph said he knew he was lucky. He had given Sara a gold bracelet with four one-quarter carrot diamonds in the middle, designed so that the gold link was between each diamond. The meaning was their family, and Sara had cried when she opened it, what a thoughtful gift. She apologized to Joseph when he had opened her sweater, which he loved. He said that the sweater took way more of her hours to knit than the gold bracelet did for him to buy. Lacey loved her cardigan. It was just a tad bit too big, but Sara was glad because that way she could wear it for another year. And MJ loved his T-shirts and book. They had a great breakfast together and worked on putting the Christmas meal in the oven.

After dinner, before going downstairs to watch a movie, they went into the living room to open the gifts from Johnny. Sara felt bad because she didn't have anything for him, but then she guessed dinner could be a gift.

MJ got another book in the series he was reading, the one behind the one that Sara gave him. Lacey got a very pretty little charm bracelet. Joseph got a nice shirt and the right size too. And Sara got some very pretty earrings. In fact, it matched the bracelet that Joseph had gotten her, something she could wear every day. The diamonds in the earrings were, she felt for sure, fake, but it was the thought that counted. Everyone loved their presents and thanked him very much for bringing them. They went downstairs to watch Bing Crosby in *White Christmas*. It was a favorite of their family.

Halfway through the movie, they paused it and had some dessert off of the table she had set up in the family room. There were not as many desserts as Thanksgiving. That was good. Johnny chose the apple pie and ice cream and helped himself to a large piece. This was the best apple pie that he had ever eaten. While they were dishing up, he told them he had found an apartment on 45th and Belmont. It had a separate bedroom and a small kitchen, and the table to eat at was part of the living room. But he was all moved in and felt that he had accomplished his goal on time, and it made him feel good.

# 24

The new year began, and school was back in session. The Christmas decorations were all down, and the first day the kids went back, Sara sat in her rocking chair in the living room and just knitted and looked out the window. She was pooped. She had worked very hard over the holidays, and now she just needed one day to take a break. She soon fell asleep and awoke a couple of hours later. She must be tired; she did not know she had fallen asleep. She had lost most of her stitches off the knitting needle. She slowly picked them up and put them on her knitting needle. She didn't want to lose them.

She got up and started working around the house. She made all the beds and picked up the laundry downstairs to the washer. Then she started a roast for dinner with red garlic mashed potatoes and green salad. She would figure out dessert once it got closer.

In the blink of an eye, it was two years later. Joseph had been promoted and, thus, spent a few more hours at work. They had celebrated their fifth wedding anniversary. Lacey was a sophomore in high school, and MJ was an eighth grader. They saw Johnny on special occasions such as Thanksgiving, Christmas, Easter, and the children's birthdays. Johnny always checked with Sara as to what book series MJ was now reading, and he was always adding to Lacey's charm bracelet.

Lacey had dates to the winter formal, sweethearts' ball, and the junior prom. She was becoming a very popular girl. Sara counted her blessings continually because both Lacey and MJ were such good kids. They never tried anything sneaky, didn't lie that she knew of and was always home by curfew times, or called if they were going to be even a few minutes late. They adjusted their dinner hour by one-half hour because of Joseph working late, and sometimes he would call and let her know that he was going to be too late to go ahead and eat. Those times brought back the old times when she and MJ would sit down to dinner by themselves.

The following year, when Lacey was a junior and MJ a freshman, winter was horrible. Every time they turned around, there was a silver thaw on the branches or snow on the ground. It was the worst consistent winter that Sara could remember. Usually, the city they lived in had mild winters—forty degrees, maybe below thirty-two, and sometimes one to two inches of snow—but this winter everything came to a standstill. Joseph tried to bring things home from work and worked from home on the dining room table. The kids, once the homework was done, would take out a puzzle and put it up on the table downstairs. Hours were taken up each day with that puzzle and then a second puzzle.

Sara always had a project going to last her through the winters, such as knitting sweaters. Stretch and Sew and polyester went by the wayside during the early 1980s. The yarn got more expensive and looked nicer; however, with the addition of Walmart stores in the area, you could buy a sweater for less than you could buy the yarn at Walmart. Often those sweaters pilled. That was the one advantage of making them, as they rarely ever pilled and got those little balls all over the sweaters.

Lacey had a boyfriend—a pretty regular one. He was such a very nice boy and so far respected Lacey and did not push her in ways she was not yet ready. His name was Tommy, and he seemed to live at the house except when there was snow or ice. His parents wouldn't let him drive, so they were on the phone forever. Lacey could work the puzzle with MJ while carrying on a telephone conversation with Tommy. When Sara got her daily work done, she would sit downstairs and knit while the kids put together a puzzle. When Lacey was on the phone, she would carry on the conversation with MJ. It was quite entertaining.

Sara fixed a large pot of split pea and ham soup for dinner. Then she made grilled cheese sandwiches. She wanted something warming in her children's stomachs for dinner. She buttered the bread, added the cheese, and wrapped it in plastic wrap, for when Joseph came home it would be ready to cook up. She kept the soup on the back-burner on low. At ten o'clock, she scooped some in a pan, put the lid on it, and put the sandwich makings both in the refrigerator. She took the rest of the soup and put it into containers she kept especially for soup. She stacked those in the refrigerator as well. She took the pan and was scrubbing it up when the doorbell rang. *Who in heaven's name is that?* Sara wondered.

She turned on the front porch light and saw it was two police officers.

"Hello, may I help you?" asked Sara.

"Yes, ma'am, are you Sara Christopher?"

"Yes, I am. Officers, what is this about?"

"May we come in? We need to talk to you."

Sara froze. She had been through this one other time in her life only it was the Marine Corps.

"Your husband, Joseph Christopher, has been in an accident. He did not die in this accident, but he is in critical condition in the hospital, ma'am. We would like to drive you to the hospital. Do you have children here?"

"Yes, wait here, I will go wake them."

Sara hurried from the room, waking MJ first and then Lacey. She told them they had to get up and get dressed very fast. Their dad had been in an accident, and police officers were here to take them to the hospital. The kids threw on their clothes, while Sara went to get all their jackets and her purse.

"Thank you for not telling me he was dead. Some years ago, the Marine Corps came to my door and told me I had lost my husband. I just don't think I can take it to have it done twice in my life," said Sara.

"Yes, ma'am," said the officer.

The kids got out to the living room in record time and put on their coats, and they all left into the police car. They crawled into the backseat, and Sara put her arms around each of the children. I asked the police officer what had happened.

"Your husband fell asleep at the wheel near as we can tell. He crossed the line and came into oncoming traffic, only at the time he crossed, there was no traffic. He hit a telephone pole on the opposite side of the road. He has very bad head injuries. The seatbelt he was wearing kept him from being thrown out of the car, but he hit his head very hard on the steering wheel."

Lacey started to cry, and MJ was very close.

"Kids, let's wait to cry when we get to the hospital and see what we are dealing with," said Sara, trying to keep to the logic. The kids were breaking a heart already broken. Just the fact that Joseph had fallen asleep at the wheel was horrible enough. They were working him too hard.

Considering the icy roads, the police officers got them there in record time. They were taken into the emergency area, and the kids were told to wait with one of the police officers, while the other one escorted Sara into the cubicle where they had been working on Joseph. His forehead looked like it had a million stitches on it. His entire face was black and blue, along with the parts of his body you could see. The first thing she did was kneel and say a prayer for his recovery.

The officer left her, and they brought her kids in. She met them in the hallway and told them they had to be very quiet. If they needed to cry, they would need to go to the hallway. It was very important that they be quiet in the room. She led them in, and you could hear both children gasp. Lacey left immediately, and MJ followed. They were out in the hallway with their arms around each other, both crying. Sara went out for a minute and put her arms around both children.

"Lacey and MJ, your dad is going to need us to be strong. He will have a lot of healing to do, and he will need us to be there for him." She left the kids and went into his room. She pulled the chair up to his bedside and held his hand. Sara stroked his hand lovingly while talking to him.

"Joseph, I am so sorry you had an accident. But you can't leave us. We need you too much. We love you too much. And I know you love us too. Joseph, I don't know if you can hear me, but I love you so much. Please, Joseph, fight to stay alive."

"Mom?" said Lacey. "Did you ask dad to fight to stay alive? Is there a possibility that he could die?"

"Yes, Lacey. He hit his head extremely hard. If his brain is bruised, or if it is bleeding, or if he has internal bleeding elsewhere, yes he could die. But he isn't because we love him and he loves us."

Lacey left the room again, and Sara could hear her out in the hallway crying again. She felt so bad she couldn't be both places at once, and right now her place was with Joseph. He must have really been sleepy to fall asleep and not wake up, even when he hit that telephone pole. Was he passed out before his accident? She would ask the doctor. If he hadn't eaten since lunch, maybe his blood sugar dropped. He was not diabetic, but can't that happen to regular humans that are not diabetic? Again, she would ask the doctor.

The bell went off at his station. She heard the nurses run in with a cart and a doctor behind her. "Code blue, Code blue," was announced over the loud speaker. They asked Sara to step outside the room. She did, but she was looking through the window. *Please, God, let him live*, she thought.

They pumped his heart and injected him with something. Then they put the paddles on. He came back once. Then they lost him again. And no matter what they did, they could not get him back again. "I love you, Joseph. I really love you and will miss you so much if you go away."

They called it at 11:32 p.m.—Joseph was gone. *Oh my God, what will I do? Oh my God, oh my God, oh my God.* She sat outside in the waiting area outside of the room and just stared like she was in shock. Her best friend had just died. This was so different than Mark. So different. She was just a kid then, and Mark could be selfish. He liked to show her off, but he treated her differently too. She loved Mark, but she adored Joseph. It was funny, not when she first married him but later on as her respect continued to grow with Joseph. She wanted to be with him the rest of her life. Now she would be alone. *I hope he was not in too much pain while he lay in the hospital and while he died*, she thought. *I wouldn't want him in pain.*

The doctor came out to talk to her and told her how sorry he was. He said that Joseph never regained consciousness since coming in. Sara asked her questions about low his blood sugar was or something else that would have caused him to be unconscious. The doctor said they would find out more when they did the autopsy. He told her that he was never in pain, and whatever had caused him to go to sleep or unconscious, he never knew. To Sara, that was a relief. She called his parents from the hospital. All she said was that he had been in an accident and asked that they come down. They came right away and were there within a half hour. When they walked in and saw Sara, they knew that their son had died. Sara ran over to them and hugged them and cried with them. She was still in shock and didn't know what to do next.

# 25

Sara and his parents arranged for the funeral. Lucy came up to the house and said, "Give me a list, and I will call all your friends and let them know. Sara handed her the Rolodex. Flowers, cards, and food arrived. Joseph did not. Johnny came over to tell her he was so sorry. He said she could count on him for any repairs, mowing the lawn, just tell him.

Sara just sat on the couch hour after hour with her arms around her children. Lacey, what was going to happen to her now? And Sara told her she wasn't going anywhere if she could help it. She loved her, and they were still a family. People dropped in to give their condolences. His boss from work came by with a check for one hundred thousand dollars for his employee life insurance. He said he was so sorry to hear about Joseph. *Me too*, thought Sara. He handed her an envelope from the office staff. They had taken up a collection. She put the envelope aside.

The funeral was held three days later. It was packed. It was very cold, and it had been hard for them to dig a grave through the ice and snow. Someone had arranged the food after the services. Maybe Lucy. She had been a godsend through this whole ordeal. People hugged her and wished her well, and she was numb. She didn't cry until every person had left. Then she let go. She cried and cried for days, possibly weeks.

About a week later, she was digging around in Joseph's things to find the bills. She knew the house payment was due, as it was the beginning of the month. She received another check from the auto insurance company. Since his death was caused by the accident, he received double the amount. It didn't make a lick of sense to her, but she didn't care; it was two hundred fifty thousand dollars. She checked with Joseph's boss to see if that same principal would apply to the insurance she received from his work. The boss checked and came back with another hundred-thousand-dollar check. "Good call," he said to her.

So she had four hundred fifty thousand dollars to last her the rest of her life. She took a look at the bills. They didn't have any credit cards; both cars were paid, and the house was paid down. The medical bills for Joseph would be paid by the auto insurance. She would keep Joseph's truck because Lacey would be driving within the next six months. She would make the monthly house payment and try to live off the interest on the total amount. She had house payment, which included the property taxes and homeowners' insurance, auto insurance, gas, and oil, other repairs as needed as well as groceries, medical, and dental bills. She really wanted to pay off the house, but what if an emergency came along? She wouldn't have the cash available. She would see how much she was earning and how much she had to live on.

She didn't want to go back to work. It was not that she was lazy by any means, but she felt that her children needed her more than ever right now all the way through school. She contacted an attorney as far as Lacey was concerned and wanted to know about adopting her or, at the least, legal guardianship. She had raised her for over six years now, and she wanted the child to feel stable. She had enough money in the checking account to last her for the next few months until she started receiving checks from the interest on her accounts.

Johnny came by one evening just to see how things were going. Sara still found herself in this very strange place. Here she was with husband number one, who had supposedly died, mourning over husband number two, who really did die. After the first week, the kids went back to school. They had paid Joseph at work for any unused vacation leave and his last payroll checks. Johnny told her to let him know if she ever needed any money, and he would take it out of his mission money. She told him she was okay. He asked her how long it had been since she was outside, and she told him it had been the day of the funeral. They had plenty of food left over, and they were eating on that.

Johnny asked her if she felt like bundling up and taking a walk around the block just to get a little fresh air. Sara agreed that would be good. The kids came along too, which was also good for them. She had told Lacey about contacting an attorney, and she would let her know what she found out.

They walked down to the corner drugstore that had a soda fountain, but instead of ice cream cones, they had hot chocolate.

"How you guys doing?" asked Johnny.

"I'm doing just okay," said Lacey. "I find it hard to concentrate sometimes, and then I find myself getting tears in my eyes. I miss him so much already!" she said as she got the tears she was talking about.

"I had a counselor in the Marine Corps tell me you must cry before you heal. One doesn't happen without the other. There are things in this lifetime that we would have never chosen, but life happens, and though we don't know the answers at the time, there is always a reason."

"You mean you're telling me that there's a reason my dad died?" said Lacey angrily.

"It is hard for you to imagine now, but yes. In essence, that is what I am saying. You may never know the reason. Maybe it is to make you a stronger person, maybe it is for your father to meet up with your mother. I don't know. I'm just guessing, and I shouldn't have said anything that deep. I'm sorry, truly I am," said Johnny.

"Well, I don't understand either, but I don't want to be mad at you, so let's just forget you said something that silly, okay?" said Lacey.

"Okay," said Johnny.

"Sara, how are you doing?" asked Johnny.

"I think I'm still in shock. I just function through the day getting whatever I need done done. But I don't do it with the same passion I used to, and that worries me," answered Sara.

"Just take it one day at a time. That's all you can do. Anything I can do to help, remember that I would like to help."

"Yeah, thanks, Johnny. I appreciate it. It's getting really cold now that the sun is going down. Let's get home and build a fire downstairs. Johnny, would you like to join us for leftovers?"

"I would love leftovers. I finally have a small kitchen, but that sure hasn't made me a better cook yet."

"Sometime when I have time, I will write down some very simple recipes for you," said Sara.

When they got home, they took out all the dibs and dabs and heated the oven. She put them in proper heating bowls and left it in the oven for thirty minutes or so. In the meantime, Johnny had gone downstairs and gotten a rip-roaring fire going. They ate at the table but took the dessert downstairs. There were several different kinds of pies and cakes. She took them out of the fridge downstairs and put them on the table, and people could choose which one they wanted or a little of all of them. They visited for a while, and then the kids said they were going to bed. She told Johnny she was going to go to bed also, as she was very tired.

He wished Sara good night and said he would check in with her in a week or two. He was being nice, not pushy, and Sara appreciated that.

The next day, she sat with the attorney and told him what she wanted. He told her that there would not be a problem adopting Lacey but that there were several reports that had to be filed first. He said the first one was with Child Services Division to make sure that there were never any reports of child abuse. Second, the grandparents would have to sign off their consent because the child was under twenty-one. Sara felt there would be no problem with either one. The third item was if there was enough money to take care of the child. Sara explained that she had four hundred fifty thousand dollars in the bank. They were in CDs earning her 5.5 percent renewable each year. She would live off the interest, and this was already set up with the bank. He felt again there would be no problem. He would get back to her soon as he had the reports in hand. She gave him the name of her bank.

She figured she would be living off two thousand one hundred dollars a month, plus both of her children were receiving social security. That was another thing she needed to check on. With both of her parents gone, would she receive more social security from her father, who had a higher wage? She would check into it. She would make do with whatever she received.

She missed him so much. She tried to get on with her life. She took walks around the neighborhood almost every day no matter how cold or how hot. She needed to get out a little bit. She would go see Lucy, and that helped her too. Lucy gave her a few more recipes, lemon bread, and chocolate peanut butter bars. She made them for the kids, and they loved them.

She was sad, then she was angry, and then she was sad again. She tried hard not to mope, but she couldn't help it.

One day, she decided she wanted to knit on her projects, so she took the knitting basket upstairs to her favorite rocking chair. It had just started to snow, and she wanted to knit and watch the snow. Snow made everything clean again. It was so pretty. She knew the kids would be home early, but that was okay. She had put a pot of chicken vegetable soup on the stove that morning and was thawing out the large yeast rolls to have alongside of it.

She dug through her knitting basket and saw the sweater that she had been knitting for Joseph for Christmas next year. It was a beautiful olive green and two shades of blue, the blues being in a stripe across his front. It was a very handsome sweater. She had gotten the front piece done and was starting to work on the back. She threw the sweater with the knitting needles attached across the room. She put her head in her hands on her lap and started crying. Here it was beautiful outside, but inside she felt like she was taking baby steps through an evil garden. She wanted Joseph back!

Joseph would want her to finish it. Joseph would want her to give it away to one of their friends. She could make that decision next year at Christmas. She set about knitting the back piece. She got very busy and didn't even hear when the kids walked in from school. They were home early because of the snow. It had already accumulated three inches and was coming down like crazy. If this continued, there would be no school tomorrow. Her children, they were everything to her now. Everything.

She got them some hot cocoa and a couple of cookies each. They asked if they could build a fire downstairs, and she said yes that would be fine. They had both been trained in the art of fire building. MJ chopped wood for her all the time. There was always plenty of kindling available, so they went downstairs with their hot cocoa, cookies, and homework. They were going to build a fire and watch it snow from down there. Sara stayed upstairs to watch it snow. The roofs were all covered and white. The snow almost covered the streets. It truly was beautiful. A clean start. Joseph would want her to live, to do things she would want to do, to be happy, to enjoy the life she was meant to have.

# 26

Spring came and then summer. She wanted to take the kids somewhere for a vacation, so she chose a resort town that was located in the central part of her state. She booked two weeks in a condo that had two bedrooms. There was a master suite with a large soaking tub right in the bedroom, a bedroom with twin beds and a bathroom off the living room with gas fireplace. There was a swimming pool on the sight and a tennis court. There were bike trails all over the resort, horseback riding, and canoeing. She thought there would be enough to keep them all busy. It had been years since Sara had been horseback riding, but she was game. They went on a long trail that went by the river a number of times. It was a beautiful ride, and the smell of pine trees was everywhere.

They rented bikes, took a picnic lunch, went up by a park, and stopped there for lunch. It was a rugged country, certainly not for the faint of heart. It was great to get out and smell fresh air. Enjoy the sunshine and take part in the activities.

They had a shopping mall of sorts and restaurants. There were also groups that played live music out in this large open area. They had Mexican food one night outside and heard the band playing. It was fun to clap along and sing some of the songs that seemed a little familiar to them. They played tennis at the condo and swam. It was lovely to almost have the pool to themselves. The kids wanted to go down to the mall shopping area and just walk around. They wanted to know if they could just go by themselves. She told them yes, but they would need to take some change and use the pay phone to check in every once and a while.

It was times like this that she wondered what she would do when the kids got out of high school. Hopefully they would go on to college. She would need to have that conversation with them soon. What would she do if she was home alone all the time when the kids were either moved out or off to college? They would come home and visit if off to college, but if they had their own apartment, she wouldn't see very much of them at all. No use feeling sorry for herself. She had lots of friends. She could volunteer. She had a ton of yard work to do all the time plus her vegetable garden and her canning. Wait, who would be there to can for if her family had moved on. Now she was grieving not only for the loss of her husband but also for the coming loss of her children.

No use to worry about it now. Maybe somewhere out there in the future she would find someone as nice as Joseph and get married again. Number three? Sara wasn't sure how she felt about that. She found herself ready to cry again, and she was just feeling sorry for herself. Sara decided to take a little bike ride by herself. She got about a mile away from the condo and took a turn, and the bike buckled. She fell and scraped her knee, and her ankle looked funny. She lay there with the bicycle on top of her. *Oh my gosh, what did I do now?* A couple went by and found her. The wife went for help, while the man got the bike off of her and tried to get her into a sitting position. Soon the Fire and Rescue team was there. She tried to tell them that her kids were at the mall and that she just thought she would take a little bike ride by herself. She missed the turn, and the bike buckled on her, and she fell.

They asked her to sit up the best she could and felt her ankle. She yelped several times, and they felt she had broken her left ankle. It was one of those freakish things where she fell just right. They took her by ambulance to the hospital in a nearby city, while one of the rescue workers went back to the condo to await a phone call from her children. He hadn't been back too long when the phone rang.

"Hello, who is this?" asked Lacey. "Did I get the right phone number?" as she compared the phone number she had with her.

"Yes, this is the resort Fire and Rescue team member. I need you to come back to the condo immediately. Your mom went for a bike ride and fell, and we think she may have a broken ankle. She was taken by ambulance to the local hospital. When you come back, I will take you to her."

The kids returned within a few minutes. They found the rescue vehicle outside and the rescue worker inside who took them immediately to join their mom. Lacey and MJ thanked him very much for his kindness. *Besides*, thought Lacey, *he's very nice to look at!*

Their mom did have a broken ankle. She felt so bad. Sara did not want to ruin their vacation, but there she was, ruining it. The rescue vehicle took her back to the condo once she was able to get her ankle wrapped. She would need to come in in a few days to have her ankle casted. They put her on painkillers for the first few days, and Lacey and MJ took care of her. She had to stay down with her leg elevated. They went up to the bookstore in the mall and picked up a few books they thought she would be interested in. They went to the grocery store and also bought magazines for her to read, something to keep her occupied. They would go out together and swim for a while, but then they were back into the condo, hating to leave her alone for very long.

She wasn't sure how they were going to get home. Lacey had her driver's permit, but she wasn't used to driving long distances and not over thirty-five miles per hour. She called Lucy, and Lucy said she would love to work it out somehow but that she had her in-laws coming for a visit. She then decided to call Johnny. Johnny asked when he should come over. School was out, so for another month, he was on vacation of sorts. He flew to the nearest city and then caught a bus to the resort area. He stayed for a few days, sleeping on the pullout couch. He took her in to get her cast put on and ordered in a pizza, which was delivered. The kids were happy to see him. It was like the pressure was off of them to be the adult person. They could be kids again, and they loved it.

He got up in the morning and fixed pancakes for everyone. Sara was now allowed out in the living room with her foot on the footstool, elevated. He waited on her hand and foot. He got her iced water, breakfast, lunch, and dinner. They watched old movies on TV together while the kids were out swimming or playing tennis. The bikes had been returned to the rental place, and they all decided they had better not push their luck. It was fun while it had all lasted, but now they needed to think about leaving in a few days.

Johnny ran the washer and dryer and got all the laundry caught up for the kids, which they packed away clean into their suitcases. No way was their mom going to be going up and down the stairs to the laundry room area for at least a few more weeks. Lacey would pitch in with MJ's help, and they would do it, but for now, it felt good to have clean clothes again. Sara was taking a nap, and Johnny ran up to the store. He wanted a barbecued steak for dinner. He didn't have a barbecue at home, and ever since he saw that sitting out on the deck, he wanted one, so he got groceries for dinner. When Sara awoke, she insisted on paying him back for some of the meals he had been making—the pizza and now steak. He said not to worry about it, but Sara did.

They had a feast for their last dinner at the condo—barbecued steak, baked potatoes, green salad, and rolls. For dessert, he had bought a fresh strawberry pie and vanilla ice cream. Yum. Serious Yum!

It was a nice night to sit out on the deck, so that was what they did. Lacey said her favorite time of the vacation was the horseback riding, and MJ said he liked all of it. He said he hoped that they could come back next summer. Sara said she also liked all of it except for breaking her ankle. She was glad that Johnny could come to their rescue and that they had a condo where there was a pool so they didn't have to pay extra for the pool. Johnny helped Sara to her bed and got the boxes out for their food to take home. He would pack the cooler in the morning. He asked Sara if she wanted him to pack her suitcase, and she said yes. If it was someone else, she would have Lacey help her, but after all, they had been married before.

When they got home and unpacked, Sara said goodbye to Johnny and thanked him over and over. She hobbled around on her crutches, and it took her a long time to get anywhere in the house. Lacey and MJ helped her quite a bit, and surprisingly Tommy helped too. She was worried about the vegetable garden after being away. The sprinklers watered everything, but the garden had weeds, the flower beds had weeds, and the lawn needed mowing. She called Johnny back and asked him if he really meant what he said about mowing the lawn. He said, "Sure did," and came over the next day. Lacey and MJ worked in the garden most of the day and got a lot of it under control. The next night and the night after and the night after that, Johnny came back until all the flower beds were weeded throughout the entire yard. He ordered in bark dust and worked through the entire weekend with both kids helping spread it. It looked really nice when they got through.

That night, he barbecued teriyaki chicken, and they had red potato salad and fresh fruit. They just had ice cream cones for dessert. It was nice to sit and look at the stars from the deck. They were all talking, and then one by one, she heard voices fading. She told the kids to go take a quick shower and then get to bed. She shook Johnny and had him go on home, but only when she knew that he was awake enough to drive. She did not want a repeat of Joseph. Again, she thanked him over and over.

# 27

The school year began, and Lacey was now a senior and MJ a sophomore. Tommy was still on the scene. They were in love and reminded Sara of her and Mark. They thought they were so grown-up, but when she looked at Lacey, she could see that they weren't. They only thought they were.

They no longer wanted the parties at Halloween, saying they were kids' stuff. Lacey was very involved in social activities during her last year of school. She went to the Sadie Hawkins dance in the fall, the winter formal around Christmas, and of course, the senior prom—all with Tommy. They talked about living at home and going to a local community college the first couple years following high school. They talked of getting married, but they wanted to wait. Sara was glad for that.

Christmas came that year, and MJ and Johnny put the outdoor lights up. They got them on the bushes, the house, and the railing on the porch. It looked really beautiful. They did a really nice job. For the inside, Johnny went with them to get their tree and put it in the stand for them. It was a very pretty noble fir, and Sara took her time decorating it. They put the artificial tree back in the basement on the table. This would be their first Christmas without Joseph. Sara had finished the sweater that she intended to give to Joseph. She thought it might be too big for Johnny, but she thought she would give it to him and explain the gift was from Joseph for helping his family out throughout the year.

The kids really wanted prime rib for Christmas dinner this year, and they wanted Sara to invite Johnny again so he wouldn't be alone on that holiday. They really liked Johnny and considered him a great friend to the family. He gladly accepted. Sara had never fixed prime rib before, so she really had to investigate how to do it. She made her scalloped potatoes to go with it, and then she made a green salad and a cranberry orange Jell-O mold, just something a little tart that would complement the meal.

They got together in the afternoon with Johnny. The morning was just for them. They were all a little melancholy with Joseph not there, and so they just wanted some time alone.

Johnny brought some packages with him and a gorgeous bouquet of white carnations, red roses, and evergreen greenery. Sara took the flowers and put them into a vase and set them on the coffee table. They really brightened up the room. He wanted us to open packages before we ate. He got MJ a radio-controlled truck. They would have fun after dinner running the thing up and down the street. Lacey opened up her package to find a beautiful heart necklace with a small diamond in it. Sara's package when she went to open it was a large box. Then there was another box inside of it. This went on for four boxes. It came down to a necklace that was not a heart but a beautiful design and had a peridot stone in the middle with matching earrings. It was beautiful, truly. Sara complained that this must have cost too much money, and he said, "What cost? It's plastic, I am sure!" Sara knew differently because she already owned plastic, and this did not look like plastic. Colored glass maybe!

Johnny opened up the sweater and got tears in his eyes when Sara told him it was from Joseph. She explained the story to him, and he liked it. He would be proud to wear it, he said. MJ had gotten him a pocket knife, and Lacey got him a flashlight plus an emergency road flasher. He really enjoyed all his gifts.

Dinner was wonderful. Her recipe for prime rib turned out fabulous—medium pink in the middle with brown edges—and the flavor was absolutely yummy. She thought scalloped potatoes would go better with the prime rib. She added asparagus and green salad, and of course, rolls. The kids had sparkling cider, and Sara and Johnny had a nice fruity white wine.

The kids said they would do the kitchen cleanup and for Mom to go put her feet up. Sometimes they swelled when she was on them too much, and they didn't want that ankle to start hurting again. Johnny brought up some of the old times, and they laughed at how silly they had been. They had been in a few classes together and remembered those teachers well.

It was a great Christmas. Johnny and Sara had a good time together. For the first Christmas since Joseph had been gone, it turned out pretty nice. Joseph was on Sara's mind a lot. He came to her in her dreams almost every night. He told her how much he loved her and how sorry he was for leaving her. Sara sometimes woke up with tears all over her face. It seemed ironic that the person she was spending a great deal of time with was a person she had previously grieved prior to Joseph.

The time flew, and soon it was spring. Sara would get out on nice days and walked the neighborhood. She loved breathing in the spring air. She loved seeing the daffodils and the tulips, which were ready to pop up, and the smell of the hyacinths. One day, when she was out for a walk, she saw a man sitting in his car who looked a great deal like Joseph. She got a chill on her neck. She thought this couldn't be happening to her again. She walked up to the car, and as she got closer, she saw that the man resembled Joseph but couldn't be him. She asked the man if his name was Joseph, and he politely answered that he wasn't. She thanked him very much and went on about her walk.

When she got home, she shared with Lacey and MJ about seeing "Joseph."

"Mom, are you going nuts?" asked Lacey.

"Well, I didn't think so, but after seeing that man, I was starting to believe so," answered Sara.

"That's okay, Mom. You have been very busy and probably have a lot on your mind," said MJ.

"I think I will get my exercise by working out in the yard. This going for a walk can be dangerous stuff," said Sara.

"Mom, did he really look like Dad?" asked Lacey.

"As a matter of fact, he did. I thought he did until he stepped out of the car and was several inches shorter than your dad, and then it made me realize that he wasn't. I'm probably doing what they say in grief recovery, that you start seeing people that look like the one you lost or will remind you of the person you lost."

When Johnny came over that night, she told him all about seeing Joseph. He laughed and said, "Oh, here you go again." Sara didn't really like him laughing at her, especially after what had happened with Johnny. Sara retaliated by hitting him on the arm.

"I didn't really look to have it start again. I just found this guy who reminded me a lot of Joseph but was several inches shorter. My first thought was, oh, here I go again, but then I realized the circumstances were totally different. You were in the service, Joseph died while driving home late at night after work. Separate circumstances. I don't think I could take it if he showed up alive. I think I would move to an isolated island where no one could find me."

The kids were downstairs doing their homework, so Johnny was able to talk freely with Sara. "Sara, I think I'm going to change my name legally to Johnny Croghan. That way, MJ will never find out the truth, and I would just as soon not have him find out, if that's okay with you."

"I didn't think I should be part of the equation of deciding. But after thinking about it, I think you're right. I don't think MJ should ever know you are his real father," stated Sarah.

"I've also done a lot of thinking about this, and I think it's for the best. I think it would overwhelm him to lose me when he was a baby before he was born and then later lose Joseph to a car accident. And then if I were to come back from the dead, I think it would devastate him he would no longer know what to trust and what not to trust. I believe in my heart this is the best thing, but I also believe that I should have my name legally changed. Can you help me decide on a middle name?"

"Well, let's see, you don't want to use Mark, Markham. Let's say your first name would be Jonathan, what could we put with that? We could use Michael, that would be pretty close. Then you would have the same initials, only reversed—MJ, JM. Jonathan Michael Croghan. Sounds pretty good to me, how about you?"

"Do you think that would be too close for comfort? Do you think he would catch on?"

"No, I don't think so. Hmm, maybe when he got older. Okay, let's think of something else. Let's go with Scott. Jonathan Scott Croghan. Sounds pretty good. What do you have to do in order to get this legalized?"

"I will file with an attorney, and he will do the paperwork. It is not known yet whether I will have to tell my reason for wanting to legalize a new name. About working for the government back in 1968. I will have to find all of that out through my attorney."

Johnny came over for dinner most every evening. After dinner, they would go outside to pull weeds, mow the lawn, and start getting the yard ready for the spring and summer season. Lacey and MJ were very busy working on the vegetable garden area.

Lacey was still dating Tommy, who was taking her to the senior prom coming up in May. Sarah and Lacey went shopping for the prom in late April. They found an ice blue dress with stones of some sort, sparkly stones, and baby seed pearls sewn on top. It was very pretty, and with Lacey's long hair, it looked gorgeous. It was a long gown, and this was the one she decided on. Tommy got a tuxedo with an ice blue tie and handkerchief for his top pocket.

The day of the prom was a warm evening. The sunset was gorgeous with pinks and oranges and purples. It would make the prom setting so nice when the kids would go out onto the deck and see this sunset. There were many parties the kids could have attended, but they chose not to. They wanted to walk along the river, hold hands, and talk about their college days and how much longer they would need to wait before they got married. Lacey was a virgin and proud of it. She wanted to wait until she was married, but that was one reason why they talked about when they would be getting married. Tommy had a good job working at a hardware facility where they made tools and nails, etc. He was still planning on attending college, however, because he knew the importance of a college education. Eighteen was just too young to get married, so they were just happy spending time together for now, and they would see where the future would take them.

MJ, being a sophomore, didn't have any proms. However, a girl from the junior class invited him to the junior prom. MJ was already over six feet tall, and he was handsome with brown hair and brown eyes. If he really looked closely into the mirror, he would see how much he resembled Johnny. He probably marked it up to a coincidence. The girl that had asked MJ out was named Dena. She had beautiful red hair and had chosen a dress of pink. MJ was not too thrilled about getting a pink tie to go with his tuxedo, but he did it for Dena. The junior prom was held on a separate night from the senior prom. Lacey put gel in MJ's hair and gave it a spiffy doo. He looked great; he was nervous, but instead of Sara driving to pick up his date, he asked Johnny if he would do it. And of course, Johnny said yes. In fact, Johnny was very flattered.

Johnny was around almost every single day or in the evening after he got done with his job. He would help Sara with the yard work, take care of the vegetable garden, can in the summertime, make jam, and even go berry picking. He was still just a family friend; he never tried anything romantic with Sara. Johnny never wanted to make Sara feel uncomfortable. He never wanted her to say to get out or leave her alone. He was thrilled he could be included in her life no matter what level.

Graduation came for Lacey, and she received an engagement ring from Tommy. She wore it proudly on her hand, even though she knew it would be two years before they would actually wed. She loved Tommy, and he loved her. She looked great in her white cap and gown, and Tommy looked great in his green cap and gown. Lacey walked across the stage proudly and had her gold rope for honor society; she was very happy. Sarah and Johnny stood and clapped when she went across the stage and then stood and clapped when Tommy also went across the stage. Afterward, they came home for a short time of cake, sparkling cider, friends, and gifts and then went back to school for the overnight party.

Sarah had planned on paying for Lacey's college and her books, so there was no need for Lacey to go out and get a job for the summer. Sarah was glad because she was really looking forward to having Lacey around. She never, for one moment, regretted adopting her, and each and every day she felt more and more like she was her daughter. Sarah had done well budgeting the original amount and living off the interest. She always knew she had backup for things such as when the roof needed replacing on the house, when the furnace went out, or when the upper deck needed to be replaced due to rotten boards. She had to use some of her reserve for such things, but that was why she hung onto it.

# 28

The summer seemed to go by so fast, and with the kids being home, there was so much more activity on a daily basis around the house. Tommy was around a lot in the evenings after work. He was not so fortunate, as his parents were not going to be paying for any of his college or books, so it would be up to him. Sara felt that it was really good for him and that it would help build character and mature him. When you have to pay for something yourself, you appreciate it more. She hoped Lacey would appreciate her college, and then she laughed to herself because she knew she would. Lacey knew the money was coming from her dad.

One day in the middle of July, there was a knock on her door. Sarah went to answer it, and there was the man that looked a lot like Joseph standing at her door. Her knees started to buckle, and she thought, *Oh my God, here we go again*. It reminded her of when Mark/Johnny had come to her door. This man introduced himself as Greg Foster. Sarah directed him to the outdoor furniture on the front porch and asked him to sit down.

"Now, Mr. Foster, what can I do for you?" asked Sara.

"Sara, you might find this hard to believe, but Joseph was my half-brother, and I would like to get to know you and Lacey because you are part of his family," said Greg.

"So how are you a half-brother? I don't understand. Does the half come from his mother or his father?"

"We shared the same father. I am older than Joseph. My father was married to my mother, and my mother died when I was very young. I was raised by my father until he met his present wife. He fell head over heels in love with her and thought she would never marry him if I was in the picture. So I was farmed out to my grandma and grandpa to be raised. When they died before Joseph was born, I was put into the foster system. That's where my last name of Foster comes from, from the family that raised me. I have tried recently getting a hold of my father, but he won't talk to me. When I told him that I was his son, he told me that his son was killed in a car accident. In other words, he doesn't want anything to do with me. Maybe he is embarrassed. When you came up to me a few months back while I was sitting in that car and asked me if I was Joseph, I knew I must have resembled him enough for you to ask me. When I got out of the car and you said, 'Oh no, my husband was much taller,' I knew I must come and tell you the story eventually."

"I am very sorry for your loss all the way around. It must have hurt that your father would not acknowledge you. Do you have other brothers and sisters?"

"Not that I am aware of. Joseph was the only one I knew of. Do you know if we have any other sisters or brothers?"

"I thought there was a half-sister, but I'm not sure if it is on the mother's side or the father's side. I could try and find out for you."

"That would be wonderful, Sara. In the meantime, would it be possible for me to meet Lacey?"

"I will have to set up a time with you for that. She has been very busy this summer with her boyfriend, Tommy. We will take your phone number where I can get a hold of you and let me find out a couple of different times that would work. Then I'll call you back and will set a date."

"That would be wonderful. I want to thank you so much for receiving me as you have with an open mind. Here is my phone number, and actually this is where I am staying right now so you can get a hold of me."

"We have a family friend by the name of Johnny who might also be here for the meeting. I hope you don't mind."

"No, that's great. I don't suppose my father would like to come? I'm sure that it would cause problems with his wife, and I'm not here to cause anyone problems. If you get a chance, you might mention it to him and let him decide for himself. I'll let you go now, Sara. Thanks again for everything."

With that, Greg went down the steps of the front porch and got into his car and drove away. She was anxious to talk to Johnny about all of this tonight when he came for dinner. She actually wanted to talk to him first before talking to Lacey. Johnny would have his antenna up about anything that would be out of the ordinary. She was probably acting paranoid. She loved MJ so much, and she loved Lacey. How could a person deny their child the right to be their child? She just couldn't understand.

When Johnny got to the house, Sara poured a glass of wine and took him out to the back deck. All the kids were downstairs, so there was no problem with them overhearing. Sara reminded him about when she saw the Joseph look-alike and then the result of Greg Foster coming to her door today. She told him that he had been abandoned by his father, Joseph's father, and would like to be able to meet Lacey and possibly meet with his father.

"So what do you think about all of this, Johnny? I would like your opinion," asked Sara.

"The one thing that pops into my mind is how he found out about Lacey. It makes me wonder if he might've had some sort of a relationship with Joseph at some point to find out that Joseph had a daughter. I think it would be okay. I would like to be there if it's okay with you, so if anything goes wrong, I could protect you and Lacey. Okay, MJ and I could protect you and Lacey."

"I knew your antenna would go up. I knew you would see something that I hadn't before. And yes, I would like it if you were here. I will try and get a hold of Joseph's father tomorrow and see what he has to say. I don't know if we could get him here without his wife. That we will have to see."

The next day, Sara got on the telephone with Mr. Christopher. He just happened to answer the phone, which she felt was her good luck. She told him that a Greg Foster had come to her door and wanted to meet Lacey and Mr. Christopher. She told Mr. Christopher that she knew the entire story and that it was not her business to judge but that she could see that Mr. Foster was hurting. Would he consider coming over tomorrow night with or without Mrs. Christopher to meet with Gregory? He told her he would think about it and give her a call back sometime during the day. He couldn't say too much; she felt that Mrs. Christopher was nearby. Before she hung up, she told him it might be nice to have a son again. He agreed with her and said he would get back to her soon.

Sara hung up the phone and went about her day. She was pickling beets from the garden, and it was a fun process. First, you cooked the beets, then took the skins off at them, then sliced them, and then put them in a pan with sugar and pickling spices. Then you heated the pan to boiling, letting it boil for a short time, and then loaded them into jars. Then you process the jars in a coldwater bath to seal them. Sara loved them on salad; with Thousand Island dressing, they were so yummy. That was her project today, and by the end of the day, she had processed twenty-one pints.

For dinner tonight, they were going to have shrimp salad, rolls, and fresh fruit for dessert with a little bit of vanilla ice cream. She would often think about Johnny, how he had blended with the family, and yet he had not pushed her romantically. She respected him for that. She was not ready for any type of romance, even with the previous husband who had come back alive. That night after dinner, they all went for a walk around the neighborhood, and even Tommy joined them. It was nice that he was around so much. Sara took Lacey's hand and explained to her about Greg Foster. She explained how she at first thought it was Joseph because they look quite a bit alike. And then she told Lacey about Greg Foster coming to the front door and explaining to Sarah who he was. He wanted to meet Lacey, and so they were trying to set something up for the next night. He also wanted to see Grandpa, and Sara had called to talk with Grandpa that day and ask if he was going to try and come over if he wasn't busy. Sara felt that was the best way to explain all of this instead of the part of Grandpa abandoning Greg when he was just little boy.

Lacey asked some questions about him. Did he really look like her dad? Was he older or younger than her dad? And where had he been all these years? Sara explained to her that she would let Greg explain and talk about it when he was ready. When they walked back through the front door, Sarah heard the phone ringing, so she ran for it. It was Mr. Christopher calling to say that yes, he would be there and that he wasn't sure if his wife would be there. He asked what time, and she told him seven o'clock. He said he would see everyone tomorrow night.

She then made a phone call to Greg Foster to let him know it was set up for the next night at seven o'clock. She also let him know that Mr. Christopher would be joining them. He was very happy, but he was very surprised.

# 29

At quarter to seven the next night, Gregory Foster stepped through the front door. He had flowers in one hand and a bottle of wine in the other. He was introduced to Johnny, and they shook hands. Sara took the wine into the kitchen, used a corkscrew, and opened it up. She was pouring glasses that were on a tray and took them into the coffee table. It seemed like only a few more minutes, and the front door bell rang again. This time, it was Mr. Christopher, also known as Grandpa. His wife was not with them. He walked in, turned to Gregory, and went to shake his hand. In return, Greg shook his hand. Okay, so it was a good start.

"Mr. Christopher, I'm not sure what to call you?" asked Greg.

"I'm not sure either. Do you mind if we hold off for a while?"

"No, that's okay."

Just then, Lacey and MJ walked into the room. Greg stood and shook her hand.

"My God, you are beautiful. I have heard you were pretty, but this I was not expecting. You must have gotten all your good looks from your mother, whom I never had the pleasure of meeting, I am sorry to say."

"Thank you, Mr. Foster. I also am not sure what to call you," said Lacey.

"Well, if you feel comfortable with calling me Uncle Greg, you may do so. If you want to wait a while, that's okay with me too, and you could just call me either Greg or Mr. Foster. I really am open," said Greg.

"You really do look like my dad," said Lacey, avoiding the subject of what to call her uncle for now.

"Yes, I have been told that time and again. The first time Joseph met me, he said it was almost like looking into a mirror except for the height. Then he knew we weren't twins, as I am several inches shorter than he was."

Mr. Christopher got a quizzical look on his face. "When did you meet Joseph?"

"It was after his first wife had died before he married Sara. It took me that long to find him. I looked long and hard, and first off I had to find his real name. Then I remembered from when I was a small boy, my last name sounded like a first name, so I looked at Stevens, at Jonathan, and then came up with Christopher," said Greg.

"Was Joseph surprised when he met you?" asked Mr. Christopher.

"Yes, but it only took one look at me to know we were related. Dad, I knew you had a good reason to hide me.

Was it that you were afraid your wife wouldn't marry you?" asked Greg.

"Gregory, first off, you know your real name is Charles. I am having a hard time with all of this." Mr. Christopher started to cry. Lacey ran to her grandpa and said, "It will be okay, Grandpa. Don't be sad."

"Thank you, dear granddaughter. I am not sad. I am…well, I guess I am sad. I am sad for all the years I lived without this man as my son. What was I thinking? I don't know, it makes me wonder about myself. I don't know where my head was. Gregory, I am so sorry for abandoning you. Can you forgive me?"

At that point, Frank Christopher grabbed his chest. "Oh my god, help me."

Sara ran to call 911, and Johnny went to grab an aspirin. He slipped the aspirin in his mouth and told him to chew it up. Sara came back and said that the ambulance was on its way.

Just as she had said that, there was a knock on the front door. The EMTs came in and started working on Mr. Christopher. They started an IV on his arm, took an EKG, and loaded him onto the gurney. Greg asked where they would be taking him. They said that he would be taken to St. Vincent Hospital since they had a wonderful cardiac unit, and Greg was going to go with him.

Lacey went up to her grandpa and gave him a kiss and a hug as gently as she could. Then she told him to get well, and she would be up to see him tomorrow. Greg gave Sara a quick hug and told her, "Thank you for setting everything up." She told him she felt really bad for her father-in-law feeling so ill. She asked that Greg call her later. She would call his wife and let her know. Whatever had not come out all those years before was certain to come out now, and that would probably be a good thing.

Greg agreed. He shook hands with Johnny and left to follow the ambulance. Once they were gone, Lacey started to cry. She was so stressed out with what had just happened in such a short time. She was scared her grandpa could die. Sara assured her that would not happen. They had gotten him medical help in short order.

She told Lacey that the only thing she could think of was it must have really struck a real chord with Mr. Christopher. He must have felt really guilty, sad, and unforgiven. It would be a good thing to have him get well and have a relationship with Greg.

Greg called later in the evening to let them know that they were keeping him overnight; they wanted to run some tests tomorrow. Mrs. Christopher was here now and knew all about Gregory, so they were having a pleasant visit. Greg said that when people got older, their values could change for the better. He was feeling welcomed for the first time in fifty years, and that was a long time to wait. He said he was spending the night with his father and that she should talk to him tomorrow before they came up, as he would be in and out of the room all day for testing.

Sara agreed that would be a good idea. The next day, she made some low-sodium, low-fat cookies made with applesauce instead of oil. They were a recipe that she had for oatmeal raisin cookies, and if you didn't know they had applesauce in them, you wouldn't know. She made a cute little basket with a note from all of them saying that when he got out of the hospital, she had more cookies in the freezer.

She had talked with Greg, and they decided that the best time for them to come up would be after dinner. When they walked in the room, she had the basket hidden from the nurses.

"These are healthy cookies. Sorry, but we all need to watch our high blood pressures, fats, and salt. Not just picking on you."

"No worries, Sara. Thank you very much for thinking of me. I didn't mean to create a scene when we were at your house."

"Oh, Frank, you did not create a scene. It was a very emotional subject and probably brought a whole set of emotions that none of us can relate to."

"Yes, that's for sure. My wife is very understanding and has agreed that the best thing for everyone concerned is that we welcome Gregory/Charles into the family and enjoy him for as long as we can have him."

"That's really great. I'm glad it all turned out well. It was such a short evening that I think Lacey may have some questions. But we'll wait until you're feeling better. I could tell her what I think, but she understands that coming from you would mean a great deal. So you let me know when you're ready for chapter two!"

"I will, Sara. Thanks for understanding. Lacey, I love you, girl, and I will answer all your questions for real."

"I know, Grandpa. I'm not in a big hurry. I'm curious, though, I won't lie."

"I appreciate you waiting."

They visited with Frank for a while and made sure he was comfortable before he left. Sara's mother-in-law, Florence, was not there. She had left to go home and take a shower. She would be back in the morning. Gregory/Charles was not going anywhere. He would go home in the morning when Florence returned for his turn at a shower and clean clothing. They were expecting to keep Frank for several more days.

Florence had suggested to Gregory/Charles that he move in with them since he was staying in a hotel at the time being. She said she was going to need help with Frank when he came home and could really use his help. She asked if he would mind if they nicknamed him Charlie since that was his original name. He said he would not mind and that he would be honored to come stay with them while he was in town. Originally, he took two weeks' vacation, but then it had already been extended once. He may just give notice. That would be something to think about. Sara was happy for him, as he needed this acceptance.

They all left the hospital and decided it would be a good night to go get an ice cream cone, so they stopped at Kell's on the way home. He didn't have a big selection, but it was always delicious ice cream. Tommy said he would buy this time. Well, there was another surprise!

# 30

The school year started for MJ, who was a junior in high school, and for Lacey a few weeks later as a freshman in college. She wasn't sure what she wanted to do when she "grew up," so she was taking general studies. MJ was old enough to get a driver's permit, and then the following October, he would be able to get his driver's license. It was hard to believe her young son was already driving; he was just growing up way too fast. He had started dating a girl by the name of Katie. She was quite cute, had dark hair and dimples, and was always in a good mood. She was part of the rally girls and was popular at school.

Lacey was still engaged to Tommy and would almost weekly turn down a date with somebody else. Sara tried to talk to her about keeping her mind open about dating other guys, but Lacey was not at all interested; Tommy was definitely the guy for her. Sara would sometimes cringe until she thought that she and Mark had been the same age when they got married. And Sara felt she was all grown-up, and so she recognized how Lacey also felt. In the community college where Lacey and Tommy were going, people were not as active socially as those who went to a regular university. There were no weekly parties, frat parties, winter formals, etc.—all that had gone by the wayside. MJ, on the other hand, was living it up with Katie. They went to the winter formal and the Sadie Hawkins dance, and they also went Christmas caroling with a big group of kids. They would have pizza parties and taco parties; they would just have a good time. He was still on honor roll, so he was not goofing off too much because he was able to keep his grades up. Sara was not sure how Katie was doing, so she decided to ask MJ one day. MJ replied that he and Katie would often study together, so MJ knew that Katie was getting her homework done.

Johnny came over one night when Sarah was making pumpkin bread and helped her. She had already made twenty loaves of zucchini bread plus zucchini relish and was very excited about getting the freezer filled up again. She loved making big pots of homemade soup and serving some sort of bread with it. Johnny was a huge help to her, but she just couldn't understand why he was not attempting romance. She did like the fact that he gave her space, gave her a chance to grieve Joseph. She really liked that about him and felt that in the long run she would want to be his friend forever.

Greg came over one day in the fall and talked about his dad. He sat down with Lacey and explained how his dad had chosen Florence over him. He explained to her how his mother had died and how Frank was so afraid he would not get the woman of his dreams if he had a child. So he at first let Greg stay with his grandma, and when the grandma died, he signed the papers to adopt Greg out.

"Grandpa feels horrible about that now. We have talked for hours and hours, and as far as I'm concerned, all is forgiven. Some of the choices we make when we are young are not ones we would make as we grow older, wiser, and more mature. Well, he should have been shopping for a mommy for me, but he was instead shopping for a lover for himself. It hurt a great deal to realize all of this, but seriously the way that your grandpa feels now, I believe him. I believe if he had to do it all over again. I would've never become Greg Foster. I would've always been Charlie Christopher."

"But, Uncle Charlie, how do you get beyond that hurt? I know what it felt like when Dad died, but then if Sara didn't want me and put me up for adoption, I would've been crushed."

"Well, Lacey, there you go. You are this beautiful little girl, and I was this ugly little boy so that's why you were chosen to not get adopted out."

"Mom, is that right?" asked Lacey.

"Not at all, Lacey. You know and I know I loved you dearly, and I was going to fight tooth and nail to be able to keep you," said Sara. "That's not saying that Frank didn't love you, Charlie. What I was willing to say, however, as he seemed quite confused, is that he loved you, but he did not give himself enough time to grieve your mother's death before he jumped into a new relationship. And then he panicked. Or so it seems to me anyway."

"I understand that, Sara, I really do. I feel that Dad and I have made huge leaps and bounds in establishing a relationship. It feels like we picked up where we left off and continued on."

"I'm really glad you two have been able to work things out. And, of course, you know that you will always be invited to every holiday we have, Christmas, Easter, birthdays, and anything else we can rummage up for an excuse for a party."

Charlie then left to go back to his home with Florence and Frank. He was going to take some getting used to being called Charlie, but he did like it; it was his name after all, and it seemed to fit him better than Greg. He had no adoptive sisters or brothers, and his mom and dad had since died before he started his search for his birth father. He would not have been able to do it otherwise; he could not hurt the family that had raised him.

Christmastime came in with Johnny there and Tommy, and they swore they would take in every possible Christmas activity they could find, such as the Pittock Mansion, which was decorated in 1890 Christmas splendor, and Peacock Lane, Portland's Christmas Street from the 1920s that annually decorates houses and yards in Christmas cheer. There was a new thing this year where they put up lots of lights around a racetrack and charged each car so much no matter how many people were inside to be able to drive around this racetrack and take in all the beautiful lights. They walked the neighborhood to see the people on their street that had put up lights. It was a beautiful sight to see. And, of course, MJ went to the winter formal with Katie. Tommy took Lacey to dinner to celebrate only having a year and a half to go before they could get married. One night, when both Lacey was out with Tommy and MJ was out with Katie, Johnny asked Sara to go to dinner just the two of them. Sara asked if there was a special occasion, and he said no; it was just the fact that the two of them could get out together.

They went to a really nice steakhouse locally in Portland, and it took them over two hours to eat dinner. It was really fun. They were able to talk about old times and clear the air once again about him being killed in action versus really being alive. They just talked and talked and talked. Afterward, they went for a drive in the car up Mount Tabor. Johnny stopped the car, and when Sara asked what he was doing, he just said he was enjoying the lights. They sat in peace and quiet for a while.

"Sara, next month, it will be three years since Joseph was killed. I have shown you how much I adore you and MJ and Lacey. I have shown you how much I am willing to help in any capacity around the house, whether it's painting or yard work, or even canning and baking. I love you, Sara Christopher. I always have, and I always will. I want to ask you if you will start dating me. I don't want to rush you, so if you're not ready, please tell me. So what do you think?"

"Well, actually, I'm a little bowled over. Johnny, I accept your proposal to date. The kids like you, and as you well know,

I do love you, but you will have to work a little hard to convince me to be in love with you again. I lost you once, and I was heartbroken, and I don't want to ever have to go through that again until we are very, very old and very, very gray."

"I agree with you, Sara. Thank you for listening to me and for accepting my proposal. The next time I make a proposal, it will have a ring attached to it. But for now, I'm happy just to be dating."

With that, he reached over and urged Sara to come to him. He first just hugged her and held her, and then he put his hand on her face and kissed her. Sara thought it was pretty wonderful. She didn't remember what it was like to be kissed like that, and especially by Johnny. Johnny had gotten his name changed. He had a confidential meeting with the judge and explained his reasoning and was granted the name, so if she ever married Johnny, she would be Sara Croghan. It was a nice name, and she appreciated him going to all that trouble for the children's sake. They drove on home, and Johnny went into the house with her. He really was quite anxious to hear how Lacey's evening had gone and how Mark Junior had enjoyed himself at the winter formal.

Sara and Johnny were sitting on the couch in the living room when Lacey came home with Tommy. She knew that as sensible of a girl that Lacey was, she would, at least, finish the next year and a half. And as Sara well knew, a lot can happen in a year and a half.

MJ came back to the house with Katie to have a little bite of dessert before he ended up taking her home. He was surprised that the only thing available for dessert was ice cream. Where was his mom's home cooking? Both MJ and Lacey were surprised to learn that Sara and Johnny had gone out to dinner alone without them. But they were happy. The kids learned that night that Sara and Johnny decided to start dating, and they got extremely excited. They really did like Johnny a great deal and were happy that he was going to become a more permanent part of their household.

Christmas Day came, and Sara and Johnny had invited Frank, Florence, Charlie, and Sara's mom and dad to come over for Christmas dinner. They were all tickled because Sara was a fairly decent cook. She had everything decorated so festively, and they felt like they were walking into a winter wonderland. Sara had made the usual turkey, dressing, mashed potatoes and gravy as well as the green beans that she had canned from her garden and cranberry sauce homemade with chunks of orange in it. In previous years, she had made rolls from a frozen dough, which rose as it thawed. This year, however, she decided to make it all from scratch and had so much fun doing it. She made a fresh apple pie and a pumpkin pie. Where she used to take shortcuts and buy premade crust, she now made it all by hand. She'd love to cook and can, and she loved her job. She may not get a regular paycheck, but it had always been such an honor to take care of MJ and Lacey in the way that she could. She really felt they also really enjoyed it because when Mother's Day rolled around, they always said so in their cards, how much they appreciated her being a stay-at-home mom and spoiling them.

Johnny had given Sara a KitchenAid mixer for Christmas, and it had a pastry hook. He sounded like he was looking forward to cinnamon rolls and pecan rolls and anything else that she could fix for him. Johnny had given Lacey a birthstone ring that she could wear on her little finger. Lacey was overwhelmed—she had Tommy's ring and Johnny's as well. For MJ, Johnny found it a little bit harder to shop for him. But he knew he liked the Chicago Bears football team, and Johnny was able to find a jersey and a football with the team logo on it. MJ loved his jersey and his football. He actually got up off the sofa and went over and gave Johnny a hug. He told Johnny that if he dated his mom long enough, he could become his dad.

"MJ, you are so silly you make me laugh," said Johnny.

"Well, you will be my new dad, and for a kid who keeps losing dads, you are taking your own life in your hands."

"What do you mean you keep losing dads?"

"My first dad, Mark, who I am named after died in Vietnam. And then Joseph and my mom got married, and he became my dad, and then he gets killed in a car accident. Now you and I look enough alike that nobody would question if we are related. But I do worry that something could happen to you. And, Johnny, I don't want anything to happen to you. Seriously, man."

"First of all, our coloring is the same, but we don't look a lot alike. I think you look more like your mother. And nothing is going to happen to me. I will be very careful, very logical, and very mature about all my decisions. One thing you have to remember is that I just asked your mom if we could start dating. We aren't getting married yet. I know you want us to, but we have to take our time. We have been friends for such a long time that to be romantically linked is going to be brand-new to us for a while. So hang in there, kid. It probably will be coming but not next week."

At that, Lacey chimed in, "Mom, you and I could have a double wedding."

"No, I don't think so, Lacey. Thank you anyway. When you get married, you may have Johnny walking down the aisle if you choose, or you might want Uncle Charlie. I do hope that you will choose Johnny. He has been such a good friend of all of us since your dad died. Besides, Lacey, when you choose to get married, it will be your special day. Everyone should be looking at beautiful you as you walk down the aisle."

"Mom, have you thought about walking me down the aisle? I know the man is supposed to walk me down, and I would love to have Johnny, but you should think about it. Things are changing in the women's world, and you are my mom. You loved me when everyone else left me."

Sara jumped up off the couch and gave Lacey a huge hug. "You know, Lacey, you were the little girl I never had. I loved you from the minute I saw you. Your dad and I went together for three years before we decided to get married, and I could feel the love for you growing in my heart every day. There was no way that any judge was going to take you away from me. I would have fought tooth and nail to get those adoption papers signed. I think if your grandparents were a little bit younger, they maybe would have fought me on it. But as it was, they knew how much I love you, so they signed off."

"And I'm glad they did, Mom. You have been the best mom in the whole wide world, and if I could get you a promise ring, I would promise to always love you and appreciate the person you are."

"My goodness, Lacey, you're going to bring tears to my eyes. We're supposed be having a fun time here opening gifts, and then have breakfast and breakfast dishes, set the table for dinner, and finish the prep for dinnertime for when our guests arrive. We just don't have time for all this blubbering," Sara said as she was wiping her eyes with a Kleenex. There was no better feeling in the world than to feel loved.

# 31

Johnny decided he wanted to take the entire family on a really nice vacation over spring break. He withdrew some money from his savings account and took the family to Hawaii. He even included Tommy and Katie. It made it more fun for everyone around. The kids were just tickled to visit the beautiful island of Oahu. One day, they rented a couple of convertibles and took a trip around the island. They stopped for lunch, watched the surfers on the north side, and took in the pineapple plantation and Pearl Harbor. It was a long day, but it was a fun day as well.

Everyone went up to their rooms to take a shower and get dressed for dinner that night. They were going to this building that rotated as the evening went on. Your table could be looking over the city, but in a short amount of time, it could be overlooking the ocean. It was really quite amazing. Johnny ordered in a sparkling cider for the under twenty-one crowd and a sparkling Spumante wine for him and Sara.

They had steak for dinner and a delicious pudding cake for dessert. After dinner, they were all so full they decided to take a walk along the beach. The evening was cooler than the daytime, but it was still about seventy degrees. You could hear the waves coming in and going out, and it was just beautiful. You could look up at the sky and see one million stars, and it was so romantic.

Sara and Johnny had one room. Lacey and Katie shared a room, and MJ and Tommy shared one. Sara knew, especially with Lacey and Tommy, this was not ideal, but it was house rules.

The next day, everyone was so tired from all the sightseeing the day before they basically just wanted to lie in the sun and swim. That was fine with Johnny and Sara. Toward evening, they all went for a walk through the international marketplace. You could hear live music coming out of the windows on the second story. It was fun to walk around and see all the beautiful jewelry, a lot of it handmade. Johnny bought Sara a set of pearl earrings, and they were lovely. They also had a small diamond attached below the pearl. It would be something that she would not only get a lot of use out of but also cherish for many, many years to come. They went to breakfast down the street the next morning and could hear the Hawaiian music playing while they ate pancakes, eggs, and sausage; it was yummy. The kids wanted to lie in the sun again, and Sara and Johnny asked the kids if they minded if they boarded the trolley, which would take them to ten different sites around the city. The kids said that it was fine and to just leave the money for lunch and have a great time. They said they would see us for dinner early later on in the evening.

Sara and Johnny boarded the trolley and had a great day of it. They had to laugh because they were getting older and just didn't want to sit in the sun all day. The kids loved to get tan, the darker the better, which showed that they had a great time on vacation. They went to various different buildings, went to the national cemetery, and then stopped and had lunch at a famous rib house. The ribs were so tender, the meat basically fell off the bone. They walked around for a little while before boarding a new trolley and did a little shopping. They also found a Mr. and Mrs. matching outfit. There was a cute sundress for her and a nice shirt for him out of matching fabric. They would wear them to the luau the next night.

When they got back from their sightseeing, they found the kids asleep on their beds. At least, they were in the right bedrooms with the right roommate. Sara was proud of her kids; she had taught them well. Sara woke them up and told them to take showers and get ready for dinner. The kids were very talkative over dinner.

"I never knew that being out in the sunshine all day could make a person so tired," said Lacey.

"Man, me neither," said Tommy.

"What was in that juice they served us?" said MJ.

"I don't know, but it was very tasty," said Tommy.

At that point, Sara and Johnny looked at each other and laughed. "Okay, so tell us this whole story. The whole story, the whole truth, so help you, God," said Johnny.

The kids all looked at each other and started to laugh themselves. "Well, how it happened was that we were all out at the pool. We had just gotten out, and the guy was walking around taking drink orders. We asked him what kind of cold juice he served, and he said he knew just the right thing to quench our thirst. Next thing we knew, we had gobbled down this drink and come to find out it must have had alcohol in it because we suddenly all got very sleepy. One of us was yawning and then the next one, so we decided to go up and take a nap. I still don't know what we drank. I'm thinking we got someone else's drinks because he knew we were not old enough. He didn't ask for ID. He just brought us drinks. We don't want you to be mad at us, and that is the honest truth," said Tommy.

"Tommy, as our future son-in-law, we trust you, and that is probably what did happen. He delivered the wrong tray to you. Can you imagine the other table that got just plain juice?" said Johnny.

At that, they all burst out laughing. Can you imagine their surprise?

They went out to dinner at a famous fish house and had delicious seafood and fish for dinner. They talked about the luau the next night, and Sara shared that she and Johnny would be dressing in their new little outfits that they bought that afternoon. The kids were all envious and decided they wanted to go shopping too. So after dinner, they did go and walked through a few shops. They also purchased matching couple outfits. It was going to be really cool.

Johnny had arranged for each of the girls to receive a lei of various orchids to match their dresses. There was something about Hawaii that is magical. Even on the island of Oahu, where it had become very commercialized, there were still areas of magic. You could be negative and look at all the commercialization, or you could be positive and enjoy the shopping, the walking, the restaurants, the ocean, the smells, the sights, the sound of the waves crashing on the shore, and the stars in the night sky. It was going to be a very fun night. On the way out to the luau, the crowd was listening to the leader at the front of the bus talk about the history and about what was going to take place that night—the beginning ceremony, the cooking of the pig, the dancers, and the flame eaters. Everyone had a great time. The guys ate so much they looked like stuffed pigs themselves. Then they sat down with dessert in front of them while the dancers and the entertainment started. Sara and Johnny held hands, as did Tommy and Lacey and Katie and MJ.

On the way home, they started out by singing some songs, but soon more and more people were asleep. Pretty soon, they turned out the bus lights, so if you were awake, you could see the lights of the city, but more than likely for the people that were sleeping. They walked from the bus depot up to their rooms and gave hugs and kisses and said, "See you in the morning. Sleep tight and don't let the bedbugs bite."

The next morning was Saturday, and they had one day left before they had to go home. The week had flown by. It had been a great week, but the kids were excited about getting back home and showing off their tans. They spent the morning after breakfast packing things they wouldn't need until they left. Then they decided they all wanted to go up to the international marketplace again for some last-minute shopping. They walked a few blocks off the main drag and found a cute restaurant decorated in 1950s. There was Elvis over in the corner, and it was Marilyn Monroe greeting you as you came in. There was a jukebox where you could choose musical numbers for five cents. They all ordered good old-fashioned cheeseburgers, french fries, and milkshakes. They didn't need to worry about being seen in their bikinis for much longer, so bring on the calories. They talked about their experiences around Hawaii, about how it was much nicer than they had anticipated. They all loved it here and would come back again in a heartbeat.

When they got back from shopping, they decided to take a quick swim at the pool. It would be their last for this particular vacation, so they lay out in the sun and swam for about three hours and then went showered and got ready for dinner. They decided to go casual that night, and so they visited the hotel restaurant right on the ocean. You could either order off the menu or take in the buffet. Of course, all the guys chose the buffet. You would think they were starving. Sara ordered a sesame chicken over rice noodles, and it was delicious. Each of the kids had their own favorites. Everybody was quieter tonight, anticipating going home tomorrow. It had been a great vacation—a memorable vacation, one that none of them would soon forget. The kids had all gotten together and figured out a gift they could give to Johnny to say thank you for the wonderful time they all had. He had unwrapped it and found it was a beautifully carved knife. The knife handle was made from Koa wood, which was native to Hawaii. He thanked everyone and gave them hugs and got tears in his eyes. He said he wanted to do something special for them because they all meant so much to him, and that was all he was going to say on the subject.

They got up the next morning, had a big breakfast, and left for the airport on the shuttle bus. They had an in-flight movie, which helped to entertain the kids, but mostly Sara slept with her head on Johnny's shoulder. She made the decision that they needed to get married. It had been awkward with her and Johnny sharing a room. The kids didn't realize that she had been married to him once before under a different name. And how could you teach your children not to sleep with each other until you're married but that she and Johnny could? So she decided she would talk to Johnny about it, and when she did, they made the decision for a summer wedding.

She would ask Lacey to be her maid of honor, and Johnny was planning on asking MJ to be his best man. They would have a small wedding, and they would invite their friends and families. So that was the next big event to plan on.

One evening, they went shopping for the wedding rings. They found this small jewelry shop in Gresham that had the most beautiful jewelry Sara had ever seen. Sara picked out a ring that she really liked. It was a gold band with four half-carat diamonds going across. They decided to get matching bands, and the nice people showed Johnny the male version of the very same ring. They decided that as they had gotten older, the very practical thing to do was to get matching bands.

They wanted to have the wedding at their house or what would become their house. It would be held in the backyard, and the reception would be outside and inside, wherever there was space. She told the kids about it the next day upon arriving home and getting things unpacked, the washing machine whirling. And she explained why she felt it was important to move up the date of the wedding. Everyone was very excited, and, of course, Sara as a planner had a list of things that needed doing. Johnny had decided to quit the janitorial job, so he was home full-time to work in the yard, to get the bark dust, and to get the vegetable garden planted and the trees and shrubs trimmed. He planted lots of beautiful red, pink, purple, blue, yellow, and white flowers throughout the whole yard. It was the most gorgeous yard they had ever seen.

Sara and Lacey went shopping for dresses. Sara chose a dress with three-quarter-length sleeves, the V-neck that came down to four very pretty and very sparkly buttons sewn on the front. The dress was white, and she was planning on wearing flowers in her hair. She got some sparkly earrings to wear, and then, of course, she would have her wedding bouquet. Lacey chose to wear pink, a very pale pink. It was beautiful on her. She was able to find some pale pink sandals that she also wore that day. The flowers they chose were very simple—white carnations and white roses for Sara and pale pink carnations and pink roses for Lacey. The guys wore slacks, vests, white shirts, and ties. Johnny's would be a white tie to match his bride, and MJ got a pale pink tie to match Lacey's.

They had taken the furniture out of the family room downstairs and had set up tables for people to eat at. There were also tables set up on the upper deck. Each table had a pink and white centerpiece and a white tablecloth, and they had rented china, glassware, and silverware so that it all matched. They also rented white chairs to go around the table. They had hired some of Katie and MJ's friends to come in and take the dirty plates upstairs to the kitchen and to make sure that there was food on the table. There were also two bottles of wine on each table—a white wine and a red wine. They cut the cake where everyone could be around them and watch them mess up each other's face with those little bits of frosting.

Then the music also began, music from the '50s, the '60s, and the '70s. The boys they had hired had taken up the white chairs where people watched the wedding, set them off to the side, and set up a wooden dance floor. The disc jockey set up in their backyard under the deck, where in case it started to rain, he would be covered. But fortunately, the weather report said beautiful sunshine. It was so much fun to dance and dance and dance. People really enjoyed themselves and stayed until the wee hours.

Sara was not going to clean up this mess tonight. So after the last guest had left, she kissed and hugged everyone including her husband and said good night. They lay in each other's arms and thanked God that things had turned out the way that they had. They had a second chance, and they were going to take it.

# 32

The following year, MJ was a senior. He had his driver's license, his own car, and, of course, his own insurance bill. Sara and Johnny told him they wanted him to maintain his National Honor Society grades and that they would pay for his insurance so he did not have to work. Lacey was in her second year of college when she had her driver's license, her own car, and, of course, her own insurance bill. Same story, they wanted her to concentrate on her grades in college instead of getting a part-time job to pay for her insurance.

Johnny's money had grown to over six million eight hundred thousand dollars. He decided he wanted to stay home and help Sara and draw a little bit of money each month from the savings account. He could live a long time without ever touching the principal amount of five million dollars. They had not taken a honeymoon, but they would. He wanted to take her on a cruise, but he needed to make sure that the kids would be okay with it; otherwise, they would take the kids with them. MJ was still dating Katie, and Lacey, of course, was still engaged to Tommy. Lacey would be twenty this coming summer and was looking forward to planning her own wedding. There was no use fighting it at this point, as they had gone together four years. They certainly knew a lot about each other by now. They seemed to be falling in love more and more each time you saw them.

Johnny helped grow the vegetables in the garden and helped Sara can them. Together they made a good team. They went grocery shopping together and prepared meals together. They took long walks together. Sometimes they would pack lunch and stop at the park down the street and have a little picnic, taking a break from working so hard. Sara got a kick out of seeing Johnny picking up the vacuum and thinking nothing of vacuuming the whole house or mopping the floors. She sat down and read a book in the daytime literally for the first time in years. While the kids were growing up, Sara kept busy most every day because of having so much to do.

Sara did get off by herself once in a while when she went down the street to visit with Lucy. They had really been through a lot together, and Sara appreciated the friendship. It was really nice to spend time with Johnny, but she was having to adjust to the 24-7, so it was a nice breather to sit down and have a chat fest with Lucy.

"Hey, girlfriend, it's good to see you. I thought that new guy kidnapped you out of the country. I haven't seen you for a while," said Lucy.

"No, just very busy canning, taking care of the yard and vegetable garden. We have been taking picnic lunches and stopping at a park for lunch. It has been fun, but we are together every hour of every day, and I miss having some alone time," replied Sara.

"Well, I have some gossip to tell you. Sandy, my daughter, is pregnant. We are sort of devastated on one side, but then we are so excited to be grandparents we can't figure out whether to be upset or not. But the thing is, it is done, and so it is what it is. We decided to be supportive of her. You know, she's the same age as Lacey."

"Is she in love with the father of the baby?" asked Sara.

"Yes, very. They will get married once the baby is born."

"See, Lucy, I don't get that. Why do people wait until after the baby is born? My goodness, don't they want to make this child legitimate?"

"Well, she wants a beautiful wedding, and we couldn't possibly get a wedding dress for a pregnant lady."

"Actually, couldn't they just get married now and have a nice reception later?"

"No, they want a church wedding. She wants to wear white. I think we should just let her have her dream."

"Lucy, is it her dream or yours?"

"Sara, why are you being so negative about this?"

"I don't think I am being negative. Just because I think that the mom and dad should be married when the baby is born. I think if she wants the wedding, she should have it. But she can't be very far along, and they make dresses that pretty much hide what is going on anyway. What I don't understand is why she's willing to have this baby out of wedlock where everyone will know but doesn't want a wedding dress that might show a small bump."

"Sara, we don't have time to plan a wedding."

"I'll help. I can sit down and dial the town if needed. Please talk to your daughter. Do you know how devastating it will be if that baby ever finds his mom and dad had not even committed themselves to each other by getting married."

"Okay, I will talk to them about it. Lots of babies are born without mom and dad not being married."

"I know, Lucy, but I really feel that this is the best thing to do."

"Fine. Let's get a list together for what they will need to do."

"One thing, if you are looking for somewhere to have it, we can have it at our house. We have a big yard, as you know, and big area downstairs. Depending, of course, on how many they would like to invite. You talk to her and let me know."

They sat and made a list of all the things that they would need to take care of and what Sara could do versus what would need to be done by the bride and her mother. They actually had fun doing it. When Sara left, she had felt good about standing up for what she believed to be right. She just hoped they loved one another enough to work things out through the years. Too many young kids today just gave up. If they didn't get their own way, they just let go of what could be a great situation for life. If they could just put a little effort into it...

That night, Lucy called Sara at home and said that she had talked to her daughter, Sandy, and that Sandy was tickled that Sara had offered her house. They would plan about fifty people to be invited. They figured out a menu, which Sara was going to prepare except for the wedding cake. They figured out that they could put this together in two weeks. They went to one of those instant printing places and got the invites printed; the next day, they were in the mail.

Lucy and Sandy went shopping for a dress and found one right away. The first one she tried on was long and lacy with a small sleeve. Sandy was thin and could wear almost anything beautifully. It was an antique white color, which would go great with antique roses. She had one maid of honor, and her groom, Bob, was going to be in just a regular light gray suit with his best man wearing the same. Bob would have a shirt and tie to match the bride, and his best man would wear a tie that would match the maid of honor. They called the rental place and had fifty chairs delivered for the front room where they would get married in front of the fireplace. The chairs would then be taken downstairs to be used around the tables. There was a gift table placed up against the wall in the hallway, and they decided to forgo the rice packets, and candies, etc. that people give at weddings. This was going to be a little more old-fashioned.

The young couple had found a small apartment to rent nearby. They also had started collecting odds and ends from people for their place. Lucy gave them Sandy's bedroom set and a couch. Other people gave a dresser, a couple of end tables, a chair, a small dining table for two or possibly four, and a couple of lamps. They figured they could go to the goodwill to fill in with what they needed.

Johnny and Sara talked about what they wanted to give as a gift to Sandy and Bob. They decided they wanted to give a check for one hundred dollars. The young kids were going to need some help, and this would be, in a way, a test. Would they use it for things they needed? Or would they blow it on fun things, a big TV, for example?

Johnny and Lucy's husband, Jerry, got together and moved all the living room furniture out to the garage and set up the chairs. Then they went downstairs and set up the tables. They put the tablecloths on the tables, and Lucy and Sandy went ahead and set the tables for fifty people. They had rented the china, glassware, and silverware like Sara had when she married Johnny. The fresh flower centerpieces that would be on each table would arrive in the morning, along with all of the other flowers. Sara had prepared potato salad, macaroni salad, baked beans, three bean salad, and roasted fried chicken. There were also a few trays of fresh fruit. She would set the fruits on the trays in the morning. It was all prepared and stored in the downstairs, along with everything else in the extra refrigerator. The buffet would be set up in the area in front of the laundry room doors. The family room had a wet bar, so it was also set up to serve drinks.

The flowers arrived the next morning, and they were beautiful. Very creative. The antique roses had silver curly things poking out, very pretty and sparkly. They would be set on a mirror square on a table cloth of antique white lace. There was also a silver bow around the base. It was very classy indeed. The maid of honor wore a light gray dress, and the best man had on a gray tie to match his suit. The flowers were basically the same theme all the way through. What a pretty wedding it was. Lacey, Tommy, and MJ and Katie helped with the food, taking it out of the fridge downstairs at the appropriate time and setting it on the table, while Sara transferred it to bowls and platters. The whole wedding was beautiful. They had the chairs arranged so that Sandy had to do sort of U—she walked down one side and then down the middle. It was a rather short aisle, but it was beautiful with flowers on the mantle and candles reflecting in the large mirror above the mantle.

The couple said their vows and had a very long and romantic kiss. Then the party started. There was no band, but MJ had put his stereo downstairs and had on a few romantic CDs while people ate dinner and then jazzed it a little after the cake. It turned out to be a very fun wedding. Both Sandy and Bob thanked Sara and Johnny over and over again. They said they would all be back the next day to help clean up—and they were. They all arrived at eight o'clock with old jeans and workshirts on. They had Bob's truck ready for the tables and chairs to be loaded and Lucy's SUV ready for the dirty tablecloths, clean dishes, stemware, and silverware to be returned. When everything was returned and cleaned up around the house and yard, the married couple, Lucy, and

Jerry came back for wedding gift opening and lunch. It was really nice to have such great friends.

The couple was astonished when they opened the card from Sara and Johnny. They had figured the wedding was enough of a gift. They were so tickled to have money for the goodwill, as there were many things they needed. The opened up a toaster, a mixer, some towels, some kitchen goodies, and many cards with money, but not as much as Sara had given them. They cleaned up their gift mess, hugged and kissed Sara and Johnny, and thanked them once again. Lucy and Jerry did the same. She said she so appreciated all that Sara had done for her Sandy. It was a beautiful wedding, one they would never forget.

The rest of the summer flew by. Lacey and Tommy had decided they both wanted to be twenty-one before getting married, so they decided to wait and have a Christmas wedding. Sara thought that was a wonderful idea because as of right now, she was a little bit "weddinged out." MJ was a freshman and Lacey a junior at the local community college. *Oh my goodness*, thought Sara. She was happy to have Johnny in her life now because once the kids left, she wouldn't be alone.

She sat down and had a talk with Johnny. She explained to him that she loved him very much but that sometimes she needed alone time. He was not to take it personally because she enjoyed every minute she had with him. She needed just a couple of hours here and there. He was glad to oblige. He said that was the hardest thing for him to get used to because he had lived alone for so many years, but he felt the same way. So they decided she would go to the library alone, and he would go to Home Depot alone. They laughed when they said their good-byes. Sara enjoyed herself, and so did Tommy. People just needed to work things out.

# 33

Christmas soon came, and not only was there the actual Christmas season itself but also a wedding. A huge wedding. This one would not be at the house. Between Lacey and Tommy, their families had come up with around two hundred fifty to three hundred guests to be invited. Invitations had been written out during Thanksgiving break and mailed that next Monday.

Lacey had five bridesmaids and one maid of honor, and of course, Tommy matched it in guys to stand up with him. The five girls wore red and carried white carnations with evergreens. The maid of honor wore white with a red bow around her middle, and of course, Lacey wore white too. The guys had a red-and-green plaid bow tie except for Tommy who wore white. It was adorable. Lacey carried white roses with greenery, and Johnny and Sara walked her down the aisle. She was such a beautiful and happy bride. They had waited four and one half years to get married, and she deserved to be happy. She had gotten all A's in her classes and was determined to continue until she got her degree. Lacey had decided she wanted to be an accountant. She had always enjoyed working with numbers, and of course working with tax law was also very important. Tommy had decided he wanted to be a history teacher, so he would need to go an additional year of schooling to get his master's.

They had found a two-bedroom apartment not too far from each of their parents' homes. Lacey was having a hard time without Sara. She had such a wonderful childhood and gave all the credit to Sara. How was she so lucky to have such a wonderful mother?

Sara, on the other hand, was having just as hard a time without Lacey. She would walk by Lacey's bedroom and just stare at the emptiness of it all. Sara decided she would paint the walls and then figure out if she wanted to put a bed in there or a crib for the someday down the road; she decided on both—a twin bed and a crib. It gave her something to do.

She selected a soft sage green and a very pretty bedspread that looked like it was a quilt. It would do nicely for a future grandson or granddaughter. For the crib, she bought a plain set of sheets and bumper pad in the sage green. Then she sat down to knit a crib-sized blanket in white and sage green. She found pictures of an A with a green apple, a B with a green balloon, and C with a brownish cat sitting on a sage green ball of yarn. If it was a girl, she would fight her urge to do pink. This was a cute grandparents' room, and she was really proud of it when she finished. Everything was brand-new, including the circular rug in browns, beiges, and sage greens with the ABCs around the outside of the circle. She showed Lacey and Tommy when they came over for dinner. Lacey said to Tommy, "No pressure, mind you," with a laugh.

After the room redecorating project, it was suddenly spring—time to work in the yard once again. Lacey had continued her classes as promised and was looking forward to graduating next year and becoming an accountant. She would work as an intern for two years under a CPA before she would be able to sign off on her own tax returns. And she was looking forward to that time.

MJ took Katie out to dinner toward the end of his freshman year. He wanted to give her a promise ring. It was a romantic evening with tablecloths on the table, candles, and low lighting. He had found one of those rings with three diamonds in it. It was supposed to represent the past, present, and future. He hoped she like it. The middle diamond was bigger than the two on the sides. He was asking her to wait until they graduated to get married, and she agreed. She loved her ring, and the size was perfect. She asked MJ whether she should wear it on her right hand or her left, and he said whichever she felt comfortable. In her excitement, she chose the left hand. It was a promise to be engaged after all. MJ took Katie home and ended the evening with a long passionate kiss. He hopped into the car a very happy camper.

He received a text from Katie as he left her saying what a wonderful evening it was and how much she loved him. She also told him that she would wait a million years for him; her love was that grand. He was reading the text when he looked up and saw headlights coming toward him. Somehow, his car had veered over into the oncoming lane. It was the last thing he remembered.

# 34

The police came to Sara's door around midnight. They told her and Johnny that MJ had been in a car accident and what hospital he had been taken to. Sara rushed to get her purse and shoes and then realized she should also probably get dressed. The police officer waited for them to get themselves ready and escorted their car as they drove themselves to the hospital. They found him in ICU. He had all sorts of tubes running around his body, but he was alive. Sara held MJ's hand.

"MJ honey, it's Mom. I'm right here. I hope you can hear me. I hope you can hear me say I love you and you need to get better. You need to wake up, honey," Sara said with tears in her eyes.

"MJ, this is Johnny. I'm here with your mom. Hey, bud, what's up? You were always such a careful driver. What happened? We both love you and want you to wake up. Wake up, MJ, wake up," Johnny said, turning to Sara. This was his only child, and though he loved Lacey, it was his only chance to have his name carried forward.

At that moment, the doctor came in to talk to them. "I am Dr. Fisher, an ER doctor here at the hospital. Can we step outside for just a moment?"

"Sure, Doctor," said Sara and Johnny together.

"Mark is doing good for what he has been through. Gratefully the other car saw him and swerved, so he missed a head-on collision. But he's pretty bruised up inside, and there is some internal bleeding. We will need to take him into surgery to discover where it is coming from. He was one lucky boy, very lucky, as it could have been much worse. We have him sleeping right now. He is not in a coma, but we wanted him to sleep to relax his body, so we could do a better examination."

"Oh, thank you, Doctor. You don't know how much that means to us. Mark, or we call him MJ, is unaware that Johnny is his father, and we hope to keep it that way, but if you need something medically, we are here to give whatever we need to save that boy's life."

"Thank you, Mrs. Croghan. By the way, that emergency card he had in his wallet was a good idea. I wish more parents would think of that, especially in this day and age of parents remarrying with different last names. In case of an emergency, contact…What a wonderful idea. Thank you for making it easier for us," said Dr. Fisher.

"You're welcome. Doctor, we love our children very much. We have a daughter we adopted and love her just as much as

MJ, and I also make her carry a card!" said Sara, taking hold of Johnny's hand.

"You are welcome to wait in his room if you would like until we take him to surgery. Then you will want to wait in the family waiting room right down the hall. It's a little more private than the general waiting room."

"We'll be here for further news, Dr. Fisher. Thank you again."

They went back into MJ's room then. Johnny got Sara settled and said he needed to call Lacey and Katie, so he stepped out of the room. He first called Lacey and apologized for waking her at this hour. He said he just wanted her to know she didn't need to come to the hospital. Lacey and Tommy said they would be down shortly.

He got Katie's mom on the phone, and she said she would go wake her. When Katie came to the phone, she sounded very sleepy. She also said she could not stay away and that she would be down shortly.

Johnny was proud of the family he had come into. MJ was important to Lacey and, of course, to Katie. By the time they arrived at the hospital, Sara and Johnny were settled in the family waiting room, as MJ had been taken to surgery. They had both arrived at the same time in the hospital parking and had walked up together. They entered the room hand in hand, crying.

"Tell us what happened. Mom, is he okay? Get us caught up." Lacey rattled her questions one after the other.

"Okay, so what the police officer told us is that he veered over into incoming traffic. They think he was distracted somehow."

"Oh my God, that's me. I sent him a text. He must have been reading it. I was thinking he would wait until he got home to read it. He had just given me this promise ring, and we were both excited. I am so sorry. Can you ever forgive me?" Katie said to the group sitting in a circle. She reached out to Sara, and Sara gave her a big hug.

"Of course, Katie. You had no idea he would read it while driving, especially after all my lecturing about texting and driving. The good news is he is going to be all right as soon as they fix where his internal bleeding is coming from. He is quite bruised, but bruises go away. He won't be able to return to school this quarter, so I will need to call his school on Monday and see what they can do for him."

"I still feel bad. I'm the one who caused the accident. What was I thinking? I should have waited until he was home to text him. It's all my fault. I'm so sorry. MJ will never forgive me, I just know it," said Katie with huge tears running down her face.

"Katie, we all love you. Now you know better to wait. Like you said, you were both excited. Can you put it aside for now? We need to concentrate on getting MJ better," said Sara in her best Mom voice.

"Yes, Mrs. Croghan," said Katie as she sat down in a corner chair.

Lacey came up and put her arm around her and whispered, "Mom's just a little crazy right now. She's just upset about MJ being in this accident. She's not mad at you."

"I know. I just need to be quiet for a while. I'll be okay, really, I will."

They all sat in the waiting room for what seemed like hours before the doctor returned. He came in through the door, removing his cap as he came.

"Mr. and Mrs. Croghan, would you please step outside for a moment?" asked the doctor.

As they both got up from their seats and followed the doctor outside the waiting room, they clung tightly to each other.

"We have a situation where we had to remove one of his kidneys, and the other one will have to be replaced, as it is badly damaged. We would like to test the entire family in the waiting room to see if we have a match first before we go outside these hospital walls."

"That sounds great to both of us," Johnny said. "Anything we can do."

"If you will please go in the room and gather the others, I will guide you to the appropriate testing station, and you can all follow me."

One by one, everyone followed the doctor down the hall, turned the corner, down the elevator by two floors, down the hall again, and finally reached the testing area. Each of them took a chair outside the curtains and waited their turn to have blood tests taken. Then it was shipped off to the lab stat.

When it was all said and done, it was Johnny who was a match. He got ready to have surgery first thing. He had to make sure he hadn't eaten for at least eight hours. They took him into MJ's hospital room, had him shower, and then gave him a hospital gown. They got him all settled into his bed, hooked up an IV to his arm, and took some more blood through the IV.

Sara stayed with both of her men through the night. She held Johnny's hand until he fell asleep naturally. Then she held MJ's hand. She fell asleep sometime in the night with her head resting on MJ's bed. Early in the morning, Sara heard MJ say, "Mom, what happened? Why am I here?"

"MJ, you were in a car accident last night. You swerved into the oncoming lane. You've been to surgery once, and you will be going again in just a little while. Johnny was a match for you, as you need a kidney, and he's going to be giving you one of his."

"That makes me sad. How did I have the accident? Why would I go into the other lane?"

"Katie was so excited about her promise ring that she texted you. You must have looked at your phone for just a moment when unknowingly you swerved into the other lane. That's all it takes, MJ, and I know you know that. You are such a good driver. You must have been excited too. I want you to know how much both Johnny and I love you and are so happy to give you anything you need. We want you to live for a very, very long time, have a healthy and happy life. So when you get ready to go to surgery, just remember you have a lot to live for. Katie loves you so much, and she's sorry she didn't wait for you to get home before she texted you."

"Can I see Katie before I go to surgery?" MJ asked his mom.

"Of course, sweetheart, I'll go get her from the waiting room. I'll be right back."

Sara ran to the waiting room, grabbed Katie by the hand, and said, "MJ wants to see you, Katie, before he's taken to surgery."

Katie grabbed her purse and then went running down the hall with Sara. They entered the room, and Sara heard Katie gasp. Sara stopped and told Katie in a whisper, "Don't let him know what he looks like right at the moment. We want him to concentrate on getting a new kidney and getting better."

"I will, I promise," she whispered back to Sara.

"Hey, MJ, sweetie, how are you doing, babe?" She approached MJ and gently kissed him and put her arms around him. Then she started to cry. "MJ, I'm so sorry I sent you that text. This is all my fault. I should have waited. I love you so much and hate to see you hurt."

"Katie, don't worry. I don't hold you responsible. I should have pulled over to read your text like I normally do. I don't know what I was thinking. You may have been the one to send the text, but you didn't make me read it while I was driving. This is my fault, not yours. Honey, please don't blame yourself. I love you, and it upsets me to see you so upset."

"MJ, I want you to see I am wearing my promise ring, and I promise to wait until you are ready to get married. I love you so much. Remember, you've got a lot to live for, honey. Someday we will get married and start a family of our own. Won't that be wonderful?"

About that time, the orderly came in to wheel Johnny to the prep area. He had already been given a relaxant. "MJ, I'll see you back at our room. I love you, boy."

"I love you too, Johnny. Thank you for the kidney."

"You're welcome, man!" Johnny gave a chuckle.

A few minutes later, the nurse came in to give MJ a relaxant. Katie kissed him good luck, and Sara gave him a kiss on the cheek. Both ladies reminded him again how much they loved him. The orderly came back and wheeled MJ to surgery, and both ladies returned to the waiting room.

Lacey had gone to the cafeteria and purchased coffee and egg sausage roll-ups and a variety of sweet rolls—a little protein, a little sugar, and a lot of caffeine. Everyone ate ravenously and then waited for the outcome of the surgeries.

Hours went by, and here came the two surgeons together. They informed the family that everything went well. MJ should be just fine when he healed from both of his surgeries, and Johnny should heal just fine being healthy and in good shape for a man his age. MJ would stay about a week before he could come home, and Johnny should be ready to go in four days. The doctors suggested they should go have dinner somewhere off campus and return in a few hours when, at that time, they would both be out of the recovery room.

Since it had been almost twenty-four hours since they had left the hospital, they all agreed that would be a good idea to do just that.

They decided to run over to a nearby restaurant that served delicious steaks and burgers. Over the next two hours, they talked about MJ and Johnny and how lucky it worked out that they were a match. Sara just bowed her head and silently thanked the Lord.

When they returned to the hospital, both guys were awake and had weak smiles on their faces. They looked rather drugged yet, and Sara had a chuckle when she saw them. She gave them both kisses and told them that she was going home to sleep in her own bed. She loved them very much and would see them tomorrow. Sara knew that MJ would start asking questions sooner or later. She thought to herself that it was definitely time to talk to him about his father. When he got better, she would set herself down with him and explain the situation.

# 35

It was weeks before Johnny and MJ had regained all their strength and felt like normal again. MJ had arranged through his college to take a medical withdrawal on his classes and signed up for the same classes come the next semester. He was now a term behind but thought he could make it up over the next couple of summers.

Life pretty much went on until one day while Johnny was at the home improvement store and MJ and Sara were alone. He came up to his Mom and said out of the blue, "Mom, is Johnny my real dad?"

"MJ, let's go into the living room where we can sit down and talk," said Sara with a heavy heart. She had hoped MJ had forgotten all about the incident when here it had come up again.

Sara sat next to MJ and took his hand into hers. "MJ, I have a true story to tell you. I'm going to ask you to hear me tell you what I need to tell you without interrupting. When I'm done, you can ask me anything within reason, okay?"

"Yes, Mom, okay."

"You weren't even born yet when two Marines came to my door and told me my husband, Mark John, had been killed. I was so sad I cried and cried and cried. I didn't want to date anyone, or even meet them. I was alone for five years, and you were my world. I took care of you day and night, and when you started school, I volunteered so I could keep my eye on you.

"I took you to the park down the road to play each afternoon, and I started to see this man that looked like your father, my husband. When I had taken a grief recovery class, one of the things they taught us was that people would look like or resemble a lost love. I started seeing people who would look like him. Each time I would approach, this man would run away.

"I had been single five years when I started dating Joseph, and we ended up getting married. Joseph became the love of my life. Mark had been the love of my life, but I finally had to get used to the fact that he was gone. Then this man came around who called himself Johnny. He was, in fact, your father. He had been hired by the US government to do a special mission, of which we may never know what it was, as it is considered top secret. He was paid five million dollars for this mission. He put the money in the bank and had never spent a dime of it. He also agreed to not contact us for ten years.

"When he did contact us, he apologized for all the trouble he had caused. He felt if he had lived through the mission, the ten years would go fast. If he had died, the five million would have been sent on to us. I was so mad at him I wasn't sure I wanted to speak to him at all, ever. Johnny begged me to allow you to see him. He wanted to be part of your life. He was so sorry he had ever done this. He really had felt that the ten years would go fast, but it didn't, and he regretted every moment of it. So he started coming around dropping in, helping out, just being with us. I loved Joseph and was not about to look at Johnny as anything else but a friend."

"When Joseph was killed in a car accident, I started to lean on Johnny a little more. He was familiar to me. He was somebody I knew, and I needed somebody. I was as heartbroken as your father. And so after a period of time, we became more than friends and started dating. And you know the rest of the story. MJ, I'm so sorry. I wanted you to know and was looking for the right time to tell you, but I guess you learned that Johnny was your father first before I could tell you. I assume the blood tests and the kidney that you needed were all the information you were looking for to figure all of this out."

"Mom, what I don't understand is why you didn't tell me a long time ago. Why did you wait until something like this to tell me, to explain it all to me? I don't get it, I really don't."

"MJ, it's kind of like telling an adopted child that they are adopted. You don't want them to love you less when they do find out, so you keep hoping for the right time, you keep putting it off, you make all kinds of excuses to yourself. And then one day, it all comes out, and the child wonders why it was kept secret so long. I don't really have an answer for you. I guess I thought it would really shock you, and maybe you weren't old enough to handle it. But the fact is, MJ, you are definitely old enough and mature enough to handle this situation. Now let me ask you what you think of Johnny being your father."

"I don't know, Mom. This is all so much to take in, but at the same time, I'm so grateful to this man for saving my life. I've always loved Johnny since the day he started coming around. I thought he was a very nice man who likes to play with his children and brought us gifts at Christmas and our birthdays, and you're always so nice to him, and I appreciated that. The one thing, Mom, it is good to give me a little time to think this thing through. I know you want me to jump up and down and yell and scream, 'Hooray, I have a dad!' How do I go tell my friends my father really is alive, after explaining all these years he was killed in Vietnam?"

"MJ, I'm not sure the important thing here is your friends. More importantly, it is how you feel. It is how your heart feels. Will it open up and love Johnny? Or will it close down and push him aside?"

"Mom, I think I love him for giving me life. Not only the beginning of life, but when he gave me his kidney, he also continued my life. I love the man. I'm just struggling with accepting him as my father. Mom, just give me some time, okay?"

Sara stood and gave her son a very large hug. She looked in his eyes and saw many things—surprise, shock, and love.

She would give her son time. And the next time she saw Lacey, she would also sit her down and tell her.

When Johnny got home from the hardware store, Sara sat him down and told them what was going on—that MJ had figured out he was his father, his real dad. She wanted everyone in the family to know what was going on now that the secret was finally out. She was also wondering if she should share the financial situation, why they didn't have to work outside the home. Johnny was actually happy that the truth came out. He wanted to go see MJ right away and talk to him, but Sara held him back and told him to give MJ some time.

Johnny got busy working on the deck, repairing the side railings and making it safer for his family to be out there. Pretty soon, MJ appeared at the door and walked over to Johnny.

"Dad, can I talk to you for a minute?" said a timid MJ to his dad.

"Why, yes, son, you can," returned a very happy dad. "Do you want to talk out here?"

"Sure, that would be okay."

"What can I help you with, son?"

"Dad, I just am trying to understand your thinking of accepting five million dollars over being with Mom and me? I guess I just remember growing up hearing her crying in her bedroom. The door would be closed, and I would knock, and she would tell me to come in, and then I would see she had all sorts of pictures of you spread on her bed and that she had been crying. How could you do that to her? You didn't know me yet, but I was a great little guy. You missed out on so much of our life, and I just can't understand why you would do it."

"MJ, when I was in Vietnam, it was the most horrible time of my whole life. There was so much shooting and killing and destruction. All I could think of was that if I could come up with a way to get out of there other than a box, it would be a good deal. I guess I was sort of brainwashed. I wanted out, that was all I could think of. When the upper echelon approached me and told me the deal, all I could think of was it was a win-win situation. If I made it out of the mission safely, ten years surely would go fast, and then we would have five million dollars. You have to remember that five million dollars in nineteen sixty-eight was like ten million now. If I didn't make it out alive, the money would go to you and your mom, which was a far cry better than ten thousand dollars they offered for those killed in action. Fortunately, I made it through the mission. I came home and started spying on your mother. I tried very hard not to let her see me. They would've taken the money away had I been found out early."

"I think I saw you at times spying on us. I've always wondered who you were. It must've been a really hard decision. Did you love my mom?"

"I love your mom so much. There were days that I thought I couldn't take it one more day without her and had to tell her. It made me realize I had not thought the whole scene through before accepting the mission. How was I going to live without her for ten years? And then when you came along, you were such a cute little baby, and you kept growing. That was so beautiful to see. I cannot tell you how many times I was sorry for that decision. I lived basically in a one-room apartment on a janitor's hours so I could save the money for you and your mom. I wanted security for your mom and for you since I had messed up our relationship, and I never thought I would get her back. But then when Joseph skidded out on the ice that night, I felt things might work differently for me in the end. It took a long time to win your mom back. I want you to know that I love you very much, and I love your mom very much, and I am so sorry, so, so sorry that I took on that mission. For other reasons besides just the money you have to understand, but I can't get into it. I can never get into it."

"What did you do when you found out Mom had married Joseph?"

"Well, I was very jealous, to be honest with you. If she had just waited two more years, we could have been together right then and there. But there was no way I could tell her about it, talk to her about it, or even let her know my presence was there. I remember one night she came running down the street, and she was screaming at me because she was fearful that I was going to harm her children. Well, in the meantime, I got the heck out of there because I didn't want her to recognize me. I think I was letting my hair grow out, and

I had a mustache and truly hoped she didn't recognize. She would look at me, like maybe she knew me from somewhere."

"Oh, that's funny, Dad."

"I think a funnier one was when she spotted me at the playground. I was hiding behind a tree, and I peeked out every once in a while and see what you were doing. You were swinging and going down the slide, and you were with Sara's help crossing the monkey bars. You were so cute. You were approximately three years old. When she saw me, she had to run back to pick you up, and when she turned around, I was already gone. I had to leave, and I didn't spy for several years after that. I just could not take a chance that she would recognize me."

"So you saw me as I was growing up?"

"Yes, every chance I could."

"I remember you were our school janitor."

"It was a way to see you, even if it was just for a moment. I loved you so much, MJ, but I couldn't be a father to you. I would go home at night and sometimes cry myself to sleep. I felt so lonely without you and Sara and again questioned what I thinking agreeing to that mission."

"I think I can understand, Dad. I want to understand, I really do. I bet it was a hard decision, and I can respect that was a difficult one for you. You probably thought that Mom would wait for you and that you would be able to walk back into her life and then everything would be fine. Instead, you lost the woman and the child you had been waiting for all those years. Well, now that you and Mom have married again and from everything I've seen you have a good relationship, now you just need your son back. Dad, I need to let you know I need to think about all of this and that I may have further questions. I just have a lot to wrap my head around right now."

"I understand, son. I really do, and you take your time. I will be here."

With that, MJ and Johnny stood at the same time and gave each other a hug. Why do secrets hurt so badly when they come out from being hidden?

# 36

When Lacey and Tommy came over the next time, Sara sat everyone down in the living room. She brought Lacey up-to-date, explaining that Johnny was really MJ's father. They also wanted to tell the children about the money, about the interest, and why they could afford to not work outside the home. Lacey and MJ laughed and said they just thought everyone was retired.

"Well, you know, kids, that the difference between staying home full-time and retirement is that you never get retired from staying at home," said Johnny, laughing back.

"I know that, but I just figured you were living off of savings," said MJ.

"We wanted you to know that the five million dollars that Johnny earned for his mission has accumulated over two million in interest. The four hundred fifty thousand dollars that Sara received from life insurance on Joseph she has learned to live off the interest very frugally while you guys were growing up. She did without a lot of things for herself so she could give to you. That is no longer the situation. Because we are married, we are now living off the interest of the five million original principal.

"We would like to buy a home in central Oregon near the Deschutes River. We want to be able to use it as a vacation home for all of us together and for anyone separately who would like to go for just a weekend. We would like your input when we go searching. I was wondering if, in two weeks when the first quarter is done, you would all be available and would feel like going over there. We could stay at the lodge, of course, in separate rooms and line up a salesperson to take us. Secondly, over and above the house, we are allowed by law to give each of you ten thousand dollars a year tax-free. We are going to start that immediately for this year and then will give you another ten thousand at the beginning of next year and so on at the beginning of each year from now on. This ten thousand is over and above your school costs. We still want you to be able to continue your schooling without having to work, and if that means that we pay for your apartment or food, car insurance, anything, then we will pay for it."

"Johnny, that is so generous of you and Mom. We could put ours in a savings account and save toward a down payment of a house. Thank you so much for your kindness. Words cannot express how excited Tommy and I are for your help. I guess we could use the money for Tommy's tuition and books."

"No, we will pay for Tommy's tuition and books. We don't want either one of you working. We want you working at going to school and finishing in a timely manner. We are able to live quite comfortably off of the interest on the five million. The ten thousand each year will come out of what is left of the four hundred fifty thousand. It's better that you both receive this as we go along and not wait until we pass on and you have to pay inheritance tax. We do, however, want you to be wise with the money, not just blow it. Lacey and Tommy, that is a great idea that you save it for a down payment on a house. Once you finish schooling and get a full-time job, you will then be able to make up your mind how much of a house payment you would be able to make each month. Your mom and I feel it is the least we can do for the children we love."

Lacey and Tommy left, and as they were driving home, Tommy said, "Lacey, wow, you have the best family in the whole world. My folks won't even help me with my tuition or books. They said if I had to work for it, I would appreciate it more in the long run. But at this point, I am getting really tired out, and might even consider quitting school to work full-time if it hadn't been for their generous offer."

"I know, Tommy. I really appreciate Mom and Johnny as my parents. Really appreciate you and love you so much as my husband. I am so very lucky we found each other and hung on to each other throughout our growing up years."

"Me too, Lacey. I don't know what I would do without you. I love you, baby girl."

"I love you too, Tommy my man."

They continued their drive home, and when they got there, they both sat down at the table to do their homework.

A college education was important to both of them, and they were determined to achieve their degrees, just like when they were waiting to get married. Lacey was really proud of her and Tommy.

# 37

The family got into the eight-passenger van and made the trip to Central Oregon. They checked into the lodge. They would meet with the real estate salesperson the next day. The overall budget was one million dollars. They hoped they could find something that would meet everyone's needs. They went to dinner at the lodge that night, and it was delicious. What a special treat.

The next day, they met up with Beth, who was their saleslady. She took them to five different homes, and they were all exhausted by the end of the day. They had a lot to talk about, as each one had some of the things one person wanted but none of the things another person wanted. One thing that Sara wanted was a private swimming pool, preferably inside because the winters could get quite snowy. They wanted five bedrooms, a large great room, a large kitchen with an eating bar, and four bathrooms, and they wanted the master bedroom to have a fireplace.

The next day, they got up, and Beth showed them the perfect house. She must have searched all night long to get everything right. They also wanted to be on the Deschutes River so that they could use their kayaks, rubber rafts, and paddle boards. Beth was able to find a five-thousand-square-foot house on the Deschutes River, and it had everything that they had asked for except the price was a little higher. The asking price was $1,100,000. At this point, Beth, Sara, and Johnny went off by themselves to make the deal. The house came fully furnished, including dishes, towels, and sheets. The fireplace was a gas fireplace in both the great room and the master bedroom, which was nice because that way they wouldn't have to get firewood in to keep the house warm. Johnny and Sara talked on the way to the real estate office and agreed that they were going to make the first offer at an even one million dollars. The owners countered at $1,050,000. Sara and Johnny recountered at $1,015,000. The owners recountered at $1,025,000, and Sara and Johnny accepted.

They went to the bank and got a cashier's check for the full amount and went back to the real estate office to close the deal. Because this was an all-cash transaction, they didn't have to wait weeks and weeks until they took ownership. It was agreed that they would all meet back here for a Christmas in Central Oregon. By then, there might be snow on the ground, and it would be a white Christmas.

Both Tommy and Katie's parents were invited to join the family sometime during this vacation. Of course, that used four of the five bedrooms, so Katie was given a bedroom and

MJ had the sleeper sofa in the loft. It worked out really well. They had a huge dining room, which sat everyone comfortably, and of course, Sara was in her element cooking for everyone. It did snow, and it was so beautiful. Everyone who came had shared their car with all their extra Christmas decorations, and everything was used. The snow was so beautiful when the sun hit it, and the families all got along well and enjoyed the time together. Sara explained that Johnny had inherited some money, and MJ and Lacey went along with the story. Sara said she felt so lucky to be able to have a beautiful home like this on the Deschutes River, and she hoped everyone would feel comfortable in sharing it with them over the years. By this time, Katie and MJ had gone together all through high school, and it was time to tell their parents about going ahead and getting married. When MJ was in that car accident, they both realized how precious life was and how it could be taken away in a second.

Both sets of parents believed it was the right thing to do; it was time. And so a June wedding was planned. As the New Year's Eve approached, they toasted the engagement with champagne. They both made a promise to each other to wait to text or pull over to read the text. As they loved each other so much, they didn't want anything happening. They talked for a while about how big of a wedding and what colors, reception, and church they wanted to get married in.

The next day, January 1, they all had to pack up and get back to town. They got ready for school, and of course, MJ and Katie had to go shopping for an engagement ring. Sara really hated to leave and was looking forward to coming back. It truly had been such a wonderful Christmas holiday. Some of them had gone skiing, while others went sledding, there was always a big pot of hot chocolate waiting for anyone to come in and get hot chocolate. Sara had taken a large coffeepot, made hot chocolate, and put it on the large island in the kitchen, along with marshmallows. Sara just enjoyed reading a book for the first time in forever by the big huge fireplace, where she also took a nap, planned the next meal, basically just enjoying herself immensely. Johnny went skiing with the kids for a while, and Sara joined in the snowball fight after dinner. It was so much fun, and she would always remember their Christmas in central Oregon. Before Sara and Johnny left, they took down all the Christmas decorations and all the laundry and then changed all the beds. It was fun to spend an extra night or two to get all the work done.

When they got home, they immediately unpacked and got the washer going. During dinner, Sara and Johnny sat down to figure out what they could do to update their home a little more. Over the next weeks, they had real hardwood floors laid throughout the whole house except for the family room downstairs where they laid new carpet. They also updated the countertops and the knobs on the kitchen cabinets and the bathroom cabinets. They put blinds, drapes, fresh paint, and fresh furniture. The house really needed it and was gorgeous when they got done. It felt good to spend a little bit of the money. They still had not touched the principal, and that was a really good feeling.

Johnny opened up a special checking account and savings account for Lacey, Tommy, Katie, and MJ. He wanted them to know, that when it came time to pay for tuition, rent, utilities, or groceries, they were covered, and he didn't have to hassle with sitting down and writing all those checks. Katie was a sophomore like MJ and was so happy to quit her job and concentrate on school. She wanted to continue her education, even after they got married. She realized they were young, but she could not imagine herself with anyone else after all these years together.

Spring came and, of course, found Sara and Johnny out working in the yard, getting the vegetable garden ready to plant. They were just enjoying the heck out of every single day. It had been really hard on Sara when Mark Senior, alias Johnny, had died, but she was now reaping the benefits.

Katie and MJ actually wanted a simple wedding. They wanted to get married at the house in Central Oregon and have a reception a couple weeks later in Portland. Sara kept asking them if they were sure, and the answer was always yes. They had fallen so much in love with the beautiful surroundings that they just wanted family and friends to be there at the wedding, and then they would invite possibly two hundred people to the reception. They decided what type of flowers they wanted, and Sara contacted the shop in Bend to get them ordered. They had chosen a date about a week after school had gotten out for the summertime. MJ had made up his lost schooling, last summer, so they were free to stay at the Central Oregon house as long as they wanted over the summer. They were both going to be juniors at the beginning of the school year in September.

MJ and Katie decided they wanted to have a waterfront reception, specifically in a restaurant on the waterfront of the Columbia River. They took over the entire restaurant and sent out the invitations before leaving to Central Oregon to get married. Johnny was to be MJ's best man, and Lacey was to be Katie's matron of honor. They housed as many as they could, and others found lodging nearby. They were married in front of the huge fireplace with candles all over the mantle and around the room. Katie had chosen a beautiful ivory gown that was kind of pioneer-looking with lace on the top sleeves to above the elbow. The cutout of the lace hung down on a very well-tanned little empire waist and then flowed down to the floor; it was Cinderella type. Katie, with her long blond hair, looked gorgeous, and she and MJ, who wore slacks and one of those little cowboy ties, looked like a really cute couple.

Sara had fixed plenty of food for the event, and of course, there were champagne and other drinks available. Everyone who came had loved the house as well; it was simply beautiful. MJ had booked a room at the lodge for their wedding night. They booked the honeymoon suite, which included a Jacuzzi tub and a fireplace.

The next day, they all returned to Sara and Johnny's to open the gifts they had received. They had gotten a two-bedroom apartment just before coming over to Central Oregon and were now going to be able to put their gifts away as soon as thank-yous were written.

MJ and Katie walked into the house. When they got inside, everyone clapped, and both Katie and MJ turned beet red. Breakfast rolls of various kinds, orange juice, coffee, and milk were on the counter, along with a tray of fresh fruit. They dished up huge plates as they were starving and sat down to eat and visit.

# 38

It was during the beautiful Portland reception that Johnny started feeling ill. He got sick to his stomach and had to excuse himself and head home. He thought he just ate something that didn't set with him, so he showered and went to bed.

The next day, Sara told him all about it, and they were so happy that both of their children had found such wonderful mates. He felt fine that day, and so they went for a long drive and stopped for lunch at a little café along the river. They sat out on the deck and watched the fisherman and the children in the river. It was a gloriously sunshiny day.

When they got home, Lacey gave them a phone call and said she would like to come over and talk to them. Sara and Johnny both said sure come on. They put a pot of decaf coffee on and set out the creamer and sugar and a plate of cookies. When Lacey got there, she was so antsy. She had a smile on her face and was dancing around like a little girl. They poured cups of coffee and went into the living room to sit down and visit comfortably.

"Mom, Johnny, I don't want you to be mad at me when I tell you this," said Lacey with a smile on her face.

"Lacey, okay, honey, just tell us what's going on," stated Sara.

"Mom, I'm pregnant. It was an accident. I was taking my pills, but still I got pregnant. I'm so happy about this, and I hope you two are also."

"Oh, honey, I couldn't be any happier. This is so exciting!"

"I was really worried to tell you and wanted to wait until after MJ's wedding. I was worried about school. It will take me longer to finish now, but I will finish."

"Lacey, I know you will. I know you are a determined person and will finish when the time is right. How does Tommy feel about all of this?"

"Tommy is really, really happy, Mom. I'm due around Valentine's Day, so that means I could continue studying until the end of this year and then take the next term off. With your help in babysitting, I should be able to go the following term, pick up some classes during the summer term, and then finish off my last year. Hopefully that will all work out. I know it will be hard to lose all those special moments with my baby, but I think I will just need to grit my teeth and bear it."

"Whatever we can do to help you, we will be there for you all the way. What a joy this is. Johnny, we are going to be grandparents. Hooray!"

Johnny came up, put her arm around Sara, and gave her a huge hug. He then went to Lacey and gave her huge hug. He said that he was so proud of his family.

Lacey got up and gave her mom a hug. Then she said she needed to get going, as she needed to get home and finish her homework. She asked them if they would like to come along when she found out the sex of the child. She also asked Johnny if she could call him Dad; she said it was time. And besides, it would be pretty hard to explain to her child that Johnny was Johnny to Mommy but was Grandpa for the little child. She felt it would make the family all complete. Of course, Johnny said he would be so proud to be called Dad.

So they fill their days with making jam and canning vegetables from the garden. They were a good team and worked well together. You could really feel that September was coming to a close as the fall nights were becoming cooler. Sara could see that Johnny lost weight and was worried about it. He said he thought it was just because he had been working so hard in the garden, mowing the lawn and taking care of the roses before winter set in. Sara said she was going to make an appointment for him at the doctor's for a physical.

The next day, she called the doctor's office, and there had been a cancellation, so she was able to get Johnny in right away.

They went to Dr. Brown's office, and he ran some tests, had some blood drawn, and said that he would get back to them as soon as all the results were in. Johnny and Sara went to dinner on the way home. They talked about how they had gotten back together, and they talked about how lucky they were in more ways than one. They had MJ, Lacey, and now a grandchild. They talked about their love for one another and how they would have never wanted to harm Joseph but that because of the accident God had brought them back together. In your life, you really only have one chance at love, but God had made sure that Sara had two. She realized how lucky she was to have found Joseph and then, when she lost Joseph, to get Johnny back.

Over the next few days, they kept busy—Johnny was working in the yard, and Sara had picked up very soft flannel and stretch terry to make little pajamas for her new grandson or granddaughter. She stopped at white, yellow, and green until she found out the gender.

On Friday, they received a telephone call from Dr. Brown. He wanted them to come into his office that afternoon so he could discuss the outcome of the lab testing. So they finished their work, showered, and went on over to Dr. Brown's office.

"Sara and Johnny, it's so good to see you," said Dr. Brown with a smile on his face. "Come in and sit down and let us talk about the results. Johnny, when you were in Vietnam, were you ever near Agent Orange?"

"Why, yes, Dr. Brown. They had just started using Agent Orange before I left Vietnam."

"What we are discovering is that Agent Orange can cause all sorts of problems—heart problems, cancer, and many others. Johnny what I have found is that you have cancer. We may be able to operate, and we may not. What I would like to do is a full body CT scan. I want to see what we are dealing with, and I want to do it right away. The fact that you have lost weight recently without changing your diet or work habits is a main factor for me to consider that you definitely have something going on inside your body. I need to be able to see inside that body so I can tell you further what is happening. You have spots on your lungs and a few on your liver. Sorry to tell you this, Johnny. So I want you to see my nurse on the way out, and I want you to make an appointment for the full body CT scan, okay?"

Sara and Johnny sat in their chairs, stunned. They had no idea that this was what they were dealing with. Of course, Johnny wanted to find out more, and he would do anything to stay alive, so they made the appointment and were actually able to get in the next day due to the emergent issue at hand.

They went home and held each other and cried. What would they do if Johnny died? What would Sara do being all alone forever? She wouldn't even consider a remarriage of any kind. They got up the next morning and went to the hospital to have the scan, and then they reported back to Dr. Brown's office on Monday morning for the results.

"Johnny, what we found on your scan is that you do have spots where we were talking previously, and we are going to start you on chemotherapy immediately if you agree," said Dr. Brown.

"Of course, Dr. Brown, whatever you say, we will do," said Sara while looking at Johnny with determination in her eyes.

The course of chemotherapy went well. He had three rounds of chemo and then one week off. He did this for three months. He lost another twenty pounds over this course, which he didn't need to lose. Sara had her blender out full-time and was making fresh banana milkshakes, fresh raspberry milkshakes (she didn't care that raspberries were out of season; she bought them anyway), anything she could make where he could absorb some calories. At about the halfway mark of chemo, they went back in to see Dr. Brown and have another CT scan. It was showing that the marks from his liver had dissolved and were gone. That was really good news. Now they just had to work on the lungs.

The kids came over and visited Johnny about every other day. In other words, they took turns—MJ was there one day, the next day would be Lacey, the next day would be MJ and so on.

In the meantime, it was time to go find out the sex of Lacey's baby. Lacey had chosen a lady doctor and was very pleased with Dr. Amanda Hoyt. They arrived at the office, which was decorated adorably with babies of animals painted on the walls; they were so cute. The walls were painted the very, very pale gray, but the paintings themselves were, of course, grass green crocodiles, black and white zebras, gray and pink baby elephants, and a wonderful giraffe. Of course, they were all babies, and it was so cute to see.

They went into the room, all four of them—Johnny, Sara, Tommy, and, of course, Lacey. Lacey got up on the table and pulled up her shirt just a smidge. Dr. Hoyt tucked the sheet inside the waistline of her long pants and pulled them down a couple of inches. Everything private was kept private. She took the warmed gel, put it on her tummy, and took the hand held device. They were all so excited about finding out if it was a boy or girl and moved it around. Johnny felt like he was going to get sick, and so he excused himself while he ran to the restroom. Everybody was saying the same thing, "Poor Johnny." The grand announcement came, and Johnny was back in the room, and everyone screamed hooray for the little girl that would be born on Valentine's Day. Sara was so excited; she had never got to use pink blankets and baby pajamas and little dresses. This child would be spoiled, Sara was sure.

On the way home from the doctor's office, Sara asked Johnny to pull over at the fabric and craft store. She went in and bought softest baby pink she could find in both yarn and fabric. She was set for a while, and it was a good time for her to work on these crafts, as it was getting very cold outside. Johnny had put the vegetable garden to rest and all the flower gardens as well.

Johnny continued his chemotherapy, and at the end of the three months, they returned to Dr. Brown's office. A CT scan had been taken prior to the appointment, and blood was already drawn for testing the number of white cells against the red cells. Or is it vice versa?

"Well, Johnny, I have some very good news for you. The spots on your lungs are nearly gone, but we are going to have to rest you for a few months before we do another round of chemotherapy. We need you to eat milkshakes and pudding and maybe some fruit pie. Anything with extra calories, as we need you to gain back at least the twenty-eight that was lost through this chemo. So you're down to about three spots and what you need to come back next month for is a chest

X-ray and a follow-up exam, and we will keep meeting like this about once a month for just about forever now. I'm sorry this had to happen to you, Johnny, but I'm very happy to give you good news."

Johnny stood and shook Dr. Brown's hand. "Dr. Brown, that is really good news. I want to live. My first grandchild is being born on Valentine's Day, and I want to be around Sara to enjoy that day. Thank you again for everything, and I'll see you next month."

Sara also stood and said, "Dr. Brown, can I give you a hug? I just feel this is wonderful news, and we will do anything we need to do to keep Johnny alive."

Sara stepped forward and told Dr. Brown, "Thank you again for the good news."

"Sara and Johnny, you are most welcome. Keep up the good work, and we'll see you in one month."

Sara and Johnny left the office with smiles on their faces, holding hands, and swinging them as they walked. They made up a little song, "I am almost cancer-free, and that makes me teehee!" They knew it was silly, but they sang it anyway because they were so happy, and they needed to share it with the world.

# 39

Time seemed to be flying way too fast. Halloween, Thanksgiving, and Christmas were all a big blur. Soon it was almost baby time. True to her word, Lacey had continued her studies until the Christmas break and then put her books down and started nesting for her baby. Katie had given her a baby shower, and it was so much fun. They used Sara's house and had pink balloons everywhere. Sara had never seen so much pink. Lacey got a lot of fun things—little tiny dresses with little tiny ruffles and pants that go under the dress with little tiny ruffles. She also got a stroller from Sara and Katie, and a few of her other friends had gone together to get her a high chair and a very cute banana hammock. Lacey had never seen one of those before and wondered how it worked. The girls explained that when you lay the baby down in the banana hammock, their backs are most comfortable and that they can sleep or play depending on how old they are. Lacey was thrilled and thanked everyone.

They enjoyed little pink and white petite fours and ice cream, having their choice between vanilla and strawberry. The girls laughed and visited and then packed up their things and went home. Then it was only Lacey and Katie left to help clean up. The girls wanted to know how Johnny was doing lately, and Sara shared with them that he was going to have to start chemo again. He was not looking forward to it, but he would do anything to stay alive.

Sari Anne was born exactly on Valentine's Day, 12:02 AM, weighing in at seven pounds and two ounces and having curly blond hair all over her adorable little head. Sara started to cry, and Johnny held her as he himself had a tear in his eye. Sara, of course, was crying for joy. She held the little girl and looked in her eyes and bonded at that very moment. It was hard for her to give the baby back to Lacey, but she knew it was very important. They stayed and visited for a while, but Johnny was getting tired out, and so they went home so he could lie down for a while. This round of chemo was really having its effects on Johnny. Sara just didn't know what she would do if she lost him.

Sara was very proud that Lacey had thought enough of her to name her child not exactly her name but a derivative so it was easier to keep them apart. She went to the hospital the next day and left Johnny home to rest. Lacey looked all beautiful and much more rested than the day before. The baby had her little pink cap on from the hospital and looked so darling wrapped in her blankets. Sari was asleep when she got there, but sometime during the visit, she awoke. After feeding her, Lacey let Sara hold the baby. Sara felt so wonderful next to this little thing. How great God was that this little individual was created and would live a wonderful life with Lacey and Tommy. She was looking forward to the time she would get to babysit when Lacey went back to school. Lacey asked how Johnny was doing, and Sara replied that he was doing pretty well but that he seemed to be tired a lot. Spring was coming, and she really worried about Johnny being able to handle the yard work without help. She was thinking of hiring a service to come in and do a lot of it. She knew Johnny would want to do the vegetable garden, and if he did that much, that would be plenty.

Lacey said to tell him that she and Tommy loved him very much and for him to hang in there. She said she would be over to see him as soon as she could. Of course, she would bring the little grandchild. Somehow, children lose their place when a grandchild is born. Grandparents are so excited to see the little one they have their arms, reaching for the child as the adult walks through the door. No hello to Lacey and Tommy but rather, "Let me see that little granddaughter of mine."

Johnny went to the doctor, and Sara went too. He took them into his office and sat him down and explained that Johnny was doing very well and wanted to know what they were doing differently. Well, he wasn't getting as much exercise, Sara explained. He seemed to be tired all the time, and he was not as sick with this chemo, just tired. He was restless, too tired to eat, too tired to sleep, too tired to read, too tired to watch TV; it just didn't make sense. They took some more tests and found that the spots were growing. Dr. Brown wanted to go in and do an exploratory surgery. He wanted to take some samples to find out exactly what was going on. Surgery was scheduled for three days from now. Johnny was to rest as much as possible, and Dr. Brown suggested that Sara and Johnny take a walk around the block at least three times a day. He said to walk around the block and then rest, walk around the block again and then rest. He wanted that so that his muscles would start building substance again.

Lacey came home from the hospital, and Johnny was getting ready to go in. What a whirlwind. Johnny went through the surgery really well, and Dr. Brown wanted them back in his office in one week's time. In the meantime, they were to keep up the schedule before the surgery—walk around the block three times a day. He was to drink milkshakes, and Dr. Brown suggested going to the health food store for some protein powder that Sara could blend in with the milkshakes. This seemed to be the only thing he could keep down when he was on chemotherapy.

MJ came home one night to talk to Lacey, and Johnny and gave them some good news: Katie was pregnant. Johnny was ecstatic; he was a grandfather to little Sari, but this time he would be a blood grandfather. Again, MJ explained it was an accident; they thought they were safe and apparently not. Katie would want to continue her schooling before and after the pregnancy, and so Sara was asked if she would be willing to babysit. The answer, of course, was yes, yes, yes. Sara would have to get another crib; she would wait to find out the sex of this child before taking on the decoration of another bedroom.

Johnny came off of the chemotherapy, and he slowly started working in the vegetable garden. Sara won the argument about the rest of the yard work, and they hired some help, who came on a regular basis. He seemed to be getting better—he was happier, loved being out in the sunshine, and moped around when it was raining. It took much longer to get things ready this year, but he was proud of his accomplishment when it was done and planted. The yard looked nice, and while they had the funds, they might as well enjoy their time together, doing what they loved and not have to worry about working in the yard. The principal of their monies had not been touched; they were living off the interest, and that was fine with them. But even if they had to touch some of the principal, that would also be okay.

Spring term, Lacey brought Sari over to stay with Grandma while she attended classes. Sara was also watching over Johnny and made sure to tuck the baby nice and snug in the stroller when Johnny and Sara took their walk around the block. Johnny looked like it was taking all his energy to get out and water the garden and take his walk. He was not the same man as before. They visited the Veterans Association to find out what would be available in the form of disabled income. When they looked them up using his personal information, they found he had died in Vietnam and, because of that, wouldn't offer any assistance whatsoever. They went home and discussed it. It was okay for them; they understood they were lucky to have quite a bit of money, and they didn't need the veterans.

The FBI knocked on Johnny's door later that day. They wanted to know why he was seeking income for a dead man. Johnny explained that he had been hired by the government to do a special mission, and since coming back, he took his middle name as his first name and his mother's maiden name as his last to keep his son from knowing he was his father. He further explained that later on, he donated a kidney to his son and that his son discovered his identity after all. After he showed proof of the income he received years ago for the mission, they dismissed the subject and left.

Johnny was really tired after all that and went to lie down and actually started to cry. He had gotten so weak and was so ashamed of the man he used to be compared to now. He was worried for Sara if he had to leave her, not financially but rather emotionally. He loved her so much and kept fighting to stay alive because of her. Now he also had a new grandson or granddaughter to the fold, one that would be of his blood.

He fell asleep and dreamed of heaven. It was so beautiful, and Jesus held out his hands to him, and he went to receive love. It was such a loving place, and Johnny felt so comfortable. All of his guilt that he had carried for years for that special mission was gone, and he felt such peace. He knew God would protect Sara, his children, his granddaughter, and his unborn grandson. In his dream, he wondered how he knew it was a grandson, but he did and felt such joy that his true name would be carried on.

Sara fixed dinner and then went in to wake up Johnny. He looked so cozy yet different, and she wondered what was going on. She tried calling to him. She shook him, and then she realized he was gone. She called 911 and explained that her husband had died and that she wanted to know what to do, whether or not they would send an ambulance. They said they would be right there. So they came in and checked on Johnny for vital signs, but they found none. Sara sat down in the chair and started to cry. She couldn't believe it. He was fighting so hard. Then he got worn out. They took him to the funeral home, and Sara was able to see him after he was prepared for burial. Lucy, her friend, came to see her and brought muffins and said she would call their friends, which she did. This would not be a military funeral, as he already had a spot for Mark Jonathan, so this one would be for Johnny Croghan. She was numb as she went through the actions of getting through this funeral. What would she do without Johnny?

The funeral was still beautiful with lots of flowers, lots of people who loved Johnny and Sara. There was food afterward at the house; somebody somehow had arranged for all of it, probably Lucy. Thank God for Lucy. Everyone said their condolences and gave her hugs, and she accepted all their well-wishes. Lucy made sure the house was all cleaned up before she left. The food was well wrapped and placed in the refrigerator as well as the desserts, which could stay on the counter.

She had a lot to look forward to—MJ's wife, Katie, having their first child that Johnny so wanted to live for and see.

She had Lacey's little girl to care for, and then when Katie delivered, she would have Katie's child to watch as they continued their education. She looked forward to many more grandchildren, even those that were still unborn, not even a twinkle in their parents' eyes as yet.

She was working in the garden weeding it and crying because she missed Johnny so much. He had planted this garden as his last loving act for Sara, and she adored him for that. It probably took all of his strength, but he did it because he loved her. She had Johnny once when he was named Mark Jonathan and lost him when he supposedly was killed in action in Vietnam. Five years later, she met Joseph and, three years after that, married him until he was killed in a car accident sliding on icy streets. And then she and Johnny had found each other in a little different situation, but it worked, and they fell in love all over again and married. Why did Vietnam have to ever happen? So many lives were lost not only during the war but since the war. These men went over and gave it their best to win a war against communism and lost. A lot of Vietnamese were also killed. What a waste of human life but not a waste to stand up for your country and fight for what you believe in.

Months later, as she was sitting by the window in her rocking chair rocking little baby Mark Jonathan III, she was thinking back over her life, holding the baby tightly and being grateful for all that God has done for her in her life. She thought of Johnny every single day, every single quart of vegetables and fruit that she canned from her garden and yard, of how Johnny used to help her and of how they would laugh and just enjoy each other. It is really a sad thing when one goes before the other and leaves the other one alone to join them in heaven at a later time.

She was glad that she had had a chance to marry Johnny and enjoy him for the rest of his life. He was, after all, the most familiar anonymous stranger she had ever known.

CPSIA information can be obtained
at www.ICGtesting.com
Printed in the USA
FSOW04n1308010816
23325FS

9 781683 190455